Text Classics

T0363043

DAVID IRELAND was born in 1927 on a kitchen table in Lakemba in south-western Sydney. He lived in many places and worked at many jobs, including greenskeeper, factory hand, and for an extended period in an oil refinery, before he became a full-time writer.

Ireland started out writing poetry and drama but then turned to fiction. His first novel, *The Chantic Bird*, was published in 1968. In the next decade he published five further novels, three of which won the Miles Franklin Award: *The Unknown Industrial Prisoner*, *The Glass Canoe* and *A Woman of the Future*.

David Ireland was made a member of the Order of Australia in 1981. In 1985 he received the Australian Literature Society Gold Medal for his novel *Archimedes and the Seagle*. He lives in New South Wales.

GEORDIE WILLIAMSON is the author of *The Burning Library*. He is the *Australian*'s chief literary critic, a position he has held since 2008, and in 2011 he won the Pascall Prize for criticism. Geordie lives with his family in the Blue Mountains.

ALSO BY DAVID IRELAND

The Unknown Industrial Prisoner
The Glass Canoe
A Woman of the Future
The Flesheaters
Burn
City of Women
Archimedes and the Seagle
Bloodfather
The Chosen

The Chantic Bird
David Ireland

Text Publishing Melbourne Australia

textclassics.com.au
textpublishing.com.au

The Text Publishing Company
Swann House
22 William Street
Melbourne Victoria 3000
Australia

First published by William Heinemann 1968
This edition published by The Text Publishing Company 2015

Cover design by WH Chong
Page design by Text
Typeset by Midland Typesetters

Printed in Australia by Griffin Press, an Accredited ISO AS/NZS 14001:2004 Environmental Management System printer

Primary print ISBN: 9781922182951
Ebook ISBN: 9781925095821
Author: Ireland, David, 1927–
Title: The chantic bird / by David Ireland ; introduced by Geordie Williamson.
Series: Text classics.
Dewey Number: A823.3

CONTENTS

Australian Psycho
by Geordie Williamson

IT WAS while working at Shell's Clyde oil refinery in Sydney during the early sixties that David Ireland, a working-class boy who left school at fifteen, began his first novel, *The Chantic Bird*. Written on note cards between Ireland's shifts operating a catalytic cracker, it remains one of the most astonishing debuts in Australian literature. Not just because of the unlikely background of its creator—the Fiercely Gifted Autodidact is a cliché—but because it is *sui generis*. No document of its time gives so distinct a sense of literary modernism adapted to local conditions.

While the everyday experience of the refinery found its way into Ireland's second novel, *The Unknown Industrial Prisoner*, *The Chantic Bird* contains the psychic residue of his time there. It's a book which suggests that wage-slavery is not a figure of speech. And it is the opening boast of Ireland's unnamed narrator, echoing the immortal first line of Joseph Furphy's *Such Is Life* ('Unemployed at last!'), that he has just been sacked from his seventeenth job 'for fighting or gambling—I don't know which—and because I was hardly ever there':

I was gambling all right, but someone called me a cheat and swung at me, I moved my head and swung back and this kid went in to one of the bosses with blood coming out of his mouth saying I was a standover man. At least the man that lectured me before they gave me my pay said I was a standover man, but he'd been a policeman before he got this good job as personnel officer, so he might have been a bit homesick for the force and a good old backhander in the friendly atmosphere of the charge room. I don't know.

Familiar ghosts hover behind these sentences: Camus' Meursault, whose moral heartbeat flatlines under a Mediterranean sun; Holden Caulfield, that mid-century archetype of wounded youth; Dostoevsky's Underground Man and his antipathy to all systems and hierarchies; and the radical freedom espoused by the American Beats. But the raw materials—gambling, fighting, sticking it to the boss—are unmistakably Australian.

This authorial voice remains thrilling and disquieting in equal measure. No one before David Ireland sounded quite like him: his writing is experimental and brutal, utterly at odds with the agrarian school of Australian fiction. And he had no immediate contemporaries, aside, perhaps, from Kenneth Cook, author of *Wake in Fright*, who was born only months after Ireland in the same south-western Sydney suburb of Lakemba. *Wake in Fright* appeared in 1961, seven years before *The Chantic Bird* was eventually published.

Today, Ireland's traces are everywhere: in the early metafictions of Peter Carey and in *The Life*, the most recent novel by Malcolm Knox; in the grungier corners of Andrew McGahan and Christos Tsiolkas; in film (*Mad Max, Ghosts...of the Civil Dead, Bad Boy Bubby*) and in the antipodean gothic of the man who may now be our most influential literary export, Nick Cave. Hemingway once suggested that all of American literature came out of *Huckleberry Finn*. It's arguable that one tradition—modernist, masculine, urban, working-class—emerged from *The Chantic Bird* and the writings that followed it, irrespective of Ireland's invisibility to the culture at large.

The narrator of Ireland's *The Chantic Bird* lives up to the self-projections of the novel's opening passage—in fact, he moves far beyond them. We first find him living in the dark recesses of Taronga Zoo, a site suggestive of the bestial heart of the ordered city. Aside from the intermittent visits the narrator makes to a suburban family, to whom his relationships are ambiguous—the three children who live there, Stevo, Chris and Allie, may be his siblings or his children; Bee, the woman who cares for them, may be a kindly domestic helper or the narrator's wife—he dwells, a feral citizen, in cracks and crevices of the urban fabric, in bushland caves or the crawl-spaces of suburban ceilings.

From these he emerges each day to enter the city and join its crowds: adopting, according to his mood and needs, the guise of merry prankster, violent criminal or domestic terrorist. His ultimate purpose is opaque. At times, the exploits he describes in a febrile mix of past and present tense are expressions of anarchy, pure and simple; at others, the narrator hints at analogies between his behaviour and the rapacity of capitalist endeavour. His antisocial actions merely parallel the violence sublimated in ordinary society. Just as Bret Easton Ellis's monstrous Patrick Bateman presents himself as an exemplary product of American late capitalism, our narrator could pass as a post-war, blue-collar Australian psycho.

Stealing televisions, torturing animals, rolling drunks, destroying property, derailing a train, committing rape and murder—youthful joie de vivre meets the empathetic dead zone of a psychopath. The moral queasiness his story engenders is turned against the reader. We are enjoined to respect the narrator's decision to drop out; we sympathise with his anger at the deadening conformity of modern life. What repels is the licence he grants himself over others in the light of those observations. The judgment he casts over his fellows is icy:

> [S]itting up in millions of houses filling in insurance policies on their fowls, their wrought-iron railings, concrete paths, light globes, their health, funeral expenses, borers, carpets, insuring against loss of work, loss of clothes, loss of conjugal rights, loss of money, loss of friends. I wonder if they had policies that could protect them from me.

The narrator employs the affectless speech of a Sydney teenager of the 1960s. Any evidence he offers is so freewheeling and colloquial that the reader is lulled into a false sense of trust. It soon becomes clear that he's unreliable on multiple levels.

We learn in the opening pages that a wannabe novelist named Petersen has approached the youth with the aim of writing his biography; these are the pages we are now reading. In this first account, there is an element of homoerotic attraction on the older man's part; later, in a different version, it seems that Petersen is mounting a therapeutic intervention into the troubled teen's life. Whatever the case, we belatedly appreciate that the story has been filtered through a second consciousness, and its emphases may be a matter of invention rather than self-exposure.

Yet the narrator assures us that he combed the text for falsehoods and exaggerations, so that it reflects true events and not Petersen's interpolated fictions. A second layer of storytelling, in other words, claims to have trumped the first.

These competing accounts destabilise the reality that the narrator has, with such relish, brought to life. Realism is ambushed in a manner as violent as the physical crimes the narrative describes. Ireland lures the reader on with a tone of easy camaraderie and by relating a vivid sequence of events. Then he turns voice and world inside out. He cuts characters to ribbons for random reassembly and designs the novel's structure to counter smooth narrative flow. It's a process that Ireland refined and expanded in his subsequent fictions.

Those novels made the author one of Australia's most awarded and controversial of the seventies and eighties. He won three Miles Franklins (for *The Unknown Industrial Prisoner*, *The Glass Canoe* and *A Woman of the Future*). A government minister intervened to revoke funding for a film based on *The Unknown Industrial Prisoner*. Another book was removed from the New South Wales school syllabus after complaints about its suitability, while a dissenting judge from the Miles Franklin panel griped that *A Woman of the Future* was 'literary sewage'.

It's hard to think of another Australian author who has been so condemned. As the country has changed—woken from its long Menzies slumber to social upheaval, integrated into a global economic order, its borders opened to diverse populations— opinion about Ireland's work has hardened. Australians have become literalists of the imagination, policing language and the reality it describes, turning away from discreditable aspects or depictions of our past in the hope of unravelling systemic inequality and oppression in the present.

Such thinking has not served a writer who has spent a long career notating his transgressive fancies. Ireland's unceasing disregard for the bounds of the acceptable and the utterable have come to be seen, at least by some, as complicity. The violence and misogyny threaded through his work must taint the texts. So it is that Ireland has remained unpublished since *The Chosen* in 1997 and was even omitted from the *Macquarie PEN Anthology of Australian Literature*.

The Chantic Bird challenges our sense of ourselves as active agents in the world. Its teenage anarchist narrator calls us on our neutrality in the face of aggression, whether social, political or economic; he decries our craving for a mediated reality, for suburban security over authentic existence. His animal delight in nature and his willingness to live for the day make him almost a hunter-gatherer whose disdain for the hierarchies and accommodations of settled society make us see them in a new light.

In an era when the west finds itself threatened by the actions of individual terrorists, *The Chantic Bird* offers us the original 'lone wolf'. The narrator's methods expose those flaws in liberal tolerance that make the punishment easier on the criminal than the crime is on the state. And he embodies the powerful resentment of those who have nothing. David Ireland's debut is a political novel which is empty of politics. But it is also a tragedy, because it is concerned with a figure whose ceaseless battles to escape society only reveal how he, too, is trapped inside it.

The Chantic Bird

1
Z O O

I'm only telling you this to let you know what a silly thing it is to live like I do. What it was, I got sacked from my seventeenth job for fighting or gambling—I don't know which—and because I was hardly ever there. I was gambling all right, but someone called me a cheat and swung at me, I moved my head and swung back and this kid went in to one of the bosses with blood coming out of his mouth saying I was a standover man. At least the man that lectured me before they gave me my pay said I was a standover man, but he'd been a policeman before he got this good job as personnel officer, so he might have been a bit homesick for the force and a good old backhander in the friendly atmosphere of the charge room. I don't know.

I don't know. If I did, do you think I'd hold back? And if you read this, Stevo, or you Chris, I want you to remember that it's sometimes better to be the one with the bloody mouth, because the sympathy you get you can often trade with.

And you, too, Allie. You might read it some day. But remember I was three months off seventeen. There must have been a lot out of work besides me, there were recruiting posters everywhere.

The way this story got written, I walked onto Pennant Hills station one morning. It was one of those times when I didn't have a car, and a long, tall streak in droopy sports clothes came up and introduced himself saying I had avid eyes, which was a pretty funny thing to say.

I would have got rid of him quick smart except that somehow he seemed to come from such a different world from me, that he didn't bother me. You won't get what I mean, I know that. But he wasn't different in a criticising sort of way and he was easy to talk to. I didn't tell him who I was; the way I see it if you're going to walk up to someone and tell him your name right off, you've got to be prepared for the other person to not tell you his name. I mean the first one that speaks is at the mercy of the one who shuts up. Can you understand that?

Anyway, he latched onto me and told me he was a writer and would I tell him about how I lived, what I did and things. I could see from the way he talked that he could see himself a famous novelist one day, taking it easy with a million dollars in his kick and calm, impressive publicity stills plastered all over the country. In every magazine.

I only tell him the things I think would be good for the readers. You can't blurt out everything. In a way I'm

4

in charge of the book and what goes into it. He can only write what I give out.

'Just put it in my words. That's the most important thing. My words. Just as I tell you.' That's what I said to him and I looked at every page to see he did it. He even put this in, how I told him what to do. So what? I wasn't getting anything out of it. Not even a penny for Stevo's coin collection.

'I'll want to see each page,' I told him. He had to show it to me page by page.

In the summer he used to sit at his little table, bare. Just about everything he did was a sort of test of me.

His name was actually David Petersen. But when I got back there with him out, I found bits of screwed-up paper with Carl Petersen, Randolph Petersen, Patric Petersen on them where he was trying out new names for himself. So he would sound successful, I guess, as well as being it. That's all I was, something to get success out of.

About getting the sack, it wasn't only being called a cheat. After all, three of us were playing odds and evens and I was working with another kid to beat the one that said I was cheating. So I suppose I was. But he had no right to be too stupid to wake up to us. The trouble is with calling people names, you can't take the words back, and if you're called you have to do something about it.

But putting us in to the boss! That was bad. He should have settled it outside, or got the other kid in with him to work against me, and paid me out that way. People at the bottom of the heap, like us, should stick together. Not call in outsiders. Bosses.

5

Even when there was no fight or argument, I still felt the same about the not sticking together. Whenever I saw a bloke trying to get above his mates I had to hack him down. Since I was a kid I've been up to here with equality and all that crap, hearing about it, I mean, not seeing it. Then in the next breath they teach you hygiene, which means that even your best friend is rotten with germs, they give you exams that show no one is equal, they give you sport so that the equal ones play for the School and the drongoes fit in nowhere, so that they're games no longer; they're a measure of something else. By the way, when I say they I mean all your teachers and parents and keepers; those sort of people. I reckon you can see from that that I'm awake up to all their bull. Not that I'm bitter about it. I just like to see people acting equal. Sometimes you have to make them do it.

I did in a lot of jobs that way. I could see the bosses didn't know what to do with me, but just the same the rest of the workers liked having me around. The day had more kick when I was there. Until each blow-up and heave-ho. At least they always laughed, even if they weren't lucky enough to get sacked with me. I don't actually have friends any more. I seem to have a habit of taking other people's friends and that's not a good thing. I'm trying to give it up. I suppose that's really why I was there at the Zoo.

After I gave up working, I lived around in any place I could get shelter, as long as no one knew where I was or who I was. I came to the conclusion that I wasn't suited to live with people, not too close to them, anyway. The truth is, I don't actually like people. Only Bee and the kids. I didn't pick on the Zoo for any reason—I just happened to think of it.

I found this good place to hide, you can find it if you look in the part south of the dingoes, north of the snakes and tigers, east of the deer. I won't tell you what it's west of, or you'll have me pinpointed.

It's lucky I can sleep anywhere. That place wasn't made for comfort.

I've started having these coloured dreams. Last night a whole dream flashed in front of my eyes and stayed there. There was no one in it, no action; that was the funny part. I was looking from out on the water onto a golden shore that bent round in half a circle. Everything else, water below and sky above, was deep brown, warm brown. The shore was one long flash of bright gold from end to end. That was all. I think I had a buzzing in the ears, but I'm not sure. It stayed a while; it didn't fade, it just turned off like a light and that was it. Only the two colours. I'd never had them in colour before.

Actually there's someone after me. I don't know who it is, or where he comes from, only that wherever I go I see him. He might be dressed differently each time but I know when I'm being followed. What saves me is I'm always on the move.

I stopped taking orders at six, when I found I could outrun Ma. I fixed the old man, too. I pepped up his tobacco with some sort of ash you get when you burn honeysuckle wood. He hated this wood on the fire, it smelled strong, but when he was yelling at me I was laughing inside: he was smoking it in his lungs. When there was no work—he used to sell insurance but the brethren didn't like that so he gave it up just when a little depression hit us; beg pardon—recession—when he couldn't get pick and shovel or process work we both used to caddy at the golf links. I had to call him Bob so no one would know he was my father.

That's just by the way, but how about that for a religion? The Plymouth Rocks, I mean. I wonder if they use insurance for their lolly factories, or if it's still sinful. Because if you watch these religions, you find that sins change. But that's not important.

What I'd like to know is, who got Ma's photos when they took her away? She was paralysed, so she couldn't have taken them. They were in a flat, wooden box, covered with flowered paper. Reddy brown. I'll tell you this, I was so mad about everything, the house and all and being the oldest and getting shunted off to work at fifteen, I went and put a handful of white ants under the house, just to give it a kick along. It was falling to pieces, but not fast enough. You know how old houses take years to die. I'm ashamed of it now, because I have to look after the house. And the kids. The others, the next oldest kids, they left when Ma left and I've got Stevo, Chris and little Allie.

I haven't actually got them. This girl, her name is Bee as far as anyone is concerned, she came to the house one day and started to do the cooking for the littlies. She wouldn't do any for me, all I had to do was get the food or the money for it and she cooked it. I don't live there, either, I only visit. Except when I hide in the ceiling. The kids started to pick up as soon as she came.

There's something the matter with me. I don't know what it is, I just have the feeling that something inside me isn't working properly. And if you notice a sort of lumpy feeling about this book, that's the way I told it. In lumps. I'm not much good at continuous work, I'm a bit stop and go.

Just the same, I'd like it to be skilful, brilliant and colourous. But what will it be at the end? A tale told by nobody.

I often think that. When the thought first struck me I went out and put the axe through the wood-bucket. In one hit. I had to bend the edges straight again later. I didn't want Bee or the kids to get cut.

Great dung-heaps are the earliest things I can remember. Heaps of horse-dung as big as mountains. That was at Rose-hill. Pinching my finger in a gate, getting lost at Manly, falling down a lot of steps, chasing a duck round the house for Christmas, looking over a fence at schoolkids, hitting a ball at Castle Hill, and Ma running about with a breadknife in her jumper screaming for the old man to put an end to her. There's nothing to do in a Zoo but lay down and remember things, once you've seen all the animals. You can go out and get tuckered up any time; there's kiosks around with stocks of food and there's the big shed where they cut up the meat for the animals.

I remember the milk tap I turned on in old Bay Road, the milko chased me all the way home and I wet my pants when he caught me. I must have been young then. I was so ashamed of it—getting caught—that I went out next day and lit the vacant block. This time there was no one to chase me, I watched the fire from the mangroves in Abbotsford Bay. The old man moved us around a lot then, one step ahead of the rent and the doctors' bills.

I can just hear the sound of a woman's dress brushing the cement. Now it's brushing the creeper growing on the walls. She's moving away. I usually stop what I'm doing when I hear someone close. And keep my mouth open. You can hear better with your mouth open. And breathe quieter. That's the way you get, like an animal, but it keeps your hidey-hole secret. Not like when old Ware dragged me out of his grapevines, the first time I was ever caught. It took me years to get even with him as he was coming home from the old Hampden Hotel, but I didn't forget. I didn't take his pay, just slammed his thick old head into a light pole. He slept on the footpath the rest of the night; they had no police patrols there.

I remember the first movie I ever saw when I was a kid, and how the horses jumped over me and how I ducked my head, down between the seats of the old Victory at Five Dock. You could smell the women's feet, with their shoes off—not exactly rotten, just sharp. The smell of some of these Zoo cages is like the smell the possums make in our roof, and the smell I caught under the big rock where I followed a porcupine with my little tommyhawk. The right name is echidna, but I like to use the name I like.

There are some ants running on the skin of old Sir Edward's cement, it's thin and you can hear anything that touches it. The rusty reinforcing wire pokes out through it in places, I like the colour of rust. There's some skin on skin, someone passing, rubbing his face maybe. It sounds like a man's face...

Lying back here thinking. These animals are no use. It's cruelty, that and the dollar sign. The first sheep I ever killed had milk in its chest, so I suppose that was cruelty too. But a man has to eat, or at least he does from a man's point of view. Dogs don't ask whether they deserve to eat. My old man had two cattle dogs, they were too big to be given names and they scared everyone for miles. I know how to kill a big dog, so they don't bother me now, but they did when I was young.

Who got the hardest hits of the horsewhip? I'll tell you who. Who had to get rid of Gyppo's pups? I did. I didn't have to shoot them, but I wanted it to be messy so the others would realise what they were getting out of, not having to do it themselves. Who had to take Gyppo along to the vet? And who had to pay the bill, with the vet writing complaining letters about having to light the furnace at midnight? It was always me. Who had to stuff up the cracks in the old man's room and burn sulphur in there to kill the germs after they took him? Me. I can remember when my only friend was our old scarred white cat, the greatest dog-scarer north of the Parramatta.

These thoughts made me miserable, so I got up and went over the wall. On the way I stopped to wave the wand about and to heave some rocks down into the bush at the south-west corner of the Zoo park. I suppose they'll have a drive against me soon.

11

When I turned seven I legally became a delinquent. Before that, all they can do is tell your mother.

I went back to the house to see Bee and the kids.

Stevo was standing in the kitchen when I got there. I waited outside to listen, like I always did. I don't believe in barging in; often you find you're not wanted.

Stevo was standing still looking at Bee. You couldn't get past that look. You'd think he was made of stone. Like a park statue. Still, it's no use making a mystery out of it, he was just a little kid and I'll be satisfied if he looks at me and takes me for what I am, too. In the kitchen I heard a cup chime. Bee always did that with her spoon on the lip of the cup. There was the sound of a greaseproof foodwrap; she must have been cutting some lunch for them for tomorrow.

When I looked back at Stevo he had a banana in his fist, peeled and sticky. He'd been washing it.

'I can't get the sticky off, Mum,' he said. 'I can't even get it off wid soap and water.' Bee grabbed the banana and washed Stevo's hands.

'I've got a headache in my tummy,' he complained, just to hog all the attention.

'Never mind your tummy. I'll get you some meddi for that.' She manipulated a brown bottle and a spoon, while he clamped his lips together.

'Say cat,' said Bee.

'I'm busy,' said Stevo, but she got the medicine down him.

'My better now,' he said after one teaspoon. 'Lollies make me better, too,' he added hopefully.

'No lollies. Bad for your teeth,' she said, like a mother. Only she wasn't his mother. After I got them out of the home at Ashfield all thin and beaten up, I told them Bee was their mother. That was good enough. I haven't finished with the keepers at that home yet. I've been picking them off one by one. Not killing, just little things like running them under, waiting for them round corners. It keeps you very busy, getting even.

The other littlies were pretty quiet. She had them eating. Stevo was still in the toilet. Bee got mad, and when she hurried him he was addressing his little old feller.

'Nice little wee-wees. Come on, little wee-wees, have some dinner.'

'Will you please get in and sit down!' she yelled. Stevo looked up at her with sympathy.

'Never mind,' he said, very understanding. 'You do poohies. You feel better when you do poohies.' She couldn't help laughing then. Neither could I, so I went in to say hullo.

I always felt a bit sorry for Stevo. There was a lot I could have told him and taught him, but the time never seemed to be right, or he had to go to bed, or have his tea. I always liked going back to the house, except that Bee seemed a bit nervous while I was there. I could never stay long. I sat on the big bed on the verandah, the one I used to sleep in with one of my brothers that died. I sat there, talking to the kids, listening to the birds' feet scrape on the iron roof. But I have to admit it, there was never really much to talk to them about, even Stevo, so I asked him about the Chantic Bird just for something to say.

13

He was full of the Chantic Bird. I asked Bee what was the strength of it, but all she'd say was that it was a story Stevo liked and he wanted to tell it to me. But I never seemed to have time to listen.

Most of the time I could do as I liked to people, as if they were stones to be thrown or bottles to be broken. Objects, that's it! Just things. But anytime I wanted I could feel what was happening to the people I damaged; anytime. I just had to let myself go and there it was, grade A sympathy just pouring out.

But hating isn't loving; you can't turn them off and on so fast, so the damage I did and the sympathy I turned on couldn't be either hating or loving.

When Bee passed close to you, there was a cool smell from her hair. It made me think of spring nights and the freesias in the grass banks by the side of the roads and the dark leaves and the scent of the pittosporum that you get when you walk round a lot at night like I do. With the smell of her in my nose I sloped out of there. I hardly recognised the sound of the underfoot stones as the sound I made; I was still on about the smell of her. It was pretty good just going in the room with her and breathing her air.

I walked away remembering the warning we'd had from one of the new people that moved in the street; they only had the story we'd given the kids, they thought we were their parents. They warned Bee, not me, about breeding like rabbits. They didn't have any kids themselves, so I don't think they worried Bee. She came from a big family, like I did. I didn't do anything to those people, it was too near home. I wasn't always there to fix any trouble.

It was dark. I passed over a spot in the yard where something moved. I just had to sneak back into the house and get my rifle and blast it, but it was only an old mother bandicoot. When I turned it over with my foot the babies were struggling to get out of it; all the skin along its stomach was torn open. For Bee's sake I trod on them and shoved them under a rock; I didn't want her to have to look at sights like that. It might put her off later when she had her own babies. She was used to me blasting away, so she didn't ask what I shot. Come to think of it, she probably thought I missed, but she didn't like to say so. Girls often think you're no good at things, when you really are.

And even if you prove it they never believe you.

Up the street I thought of my old grandmother and how she used to walk miles, when she was alive, just to get apples a bit cheaper. That took me back to my great-grandfather who was supposed to have got his eye torn out in a fight in Pitt Street and clapped it back in his head and chased the man that did it. That was before this century. My old man told me that one. We still had the eye in the family, because when he had to get a glass eye—the other one was never any good even though he clapped it back in—he put his real eye in a bottle with some metho before it went bad. It's still in the family. You have to change the metho now and again. At least they told us kids it was the same eye. The others may have got Ma's photos but I got the eye.

I'd been dawdling along, until I suddenly found myself running. That was me, running or dawdling. I could keep running for a long time. I felt pretty strong. There was rain, grizzling in the gutters and getting guzzled down the drains.

I get ideas when I'm running. The idea I got this time was to do what I'd seen two men in Hyde Park doing. One sort of kept looking around while the other one knelt down by this sailor who was drunk, and turned him over gently and took all the money out of his pockets and the watch off his wrist and a ring off his finger that had a square black stone in it. I was only a small child when I saw that, but it made a big impression on me. It looked such an easy way to get something for nothing. So what I did, I waited outside the old Railway Hotel at Hornsby—it was a bit of a blood-house then before they knocked it down and built it up again—until closing time. I saw a prospect picking his way carefully and at great length down the top steps to the foot-path. He wasn't out of the pub fifty yards before he wanted to use the gutter as a toilet. I was behind him, but just as I hit him his head rolled to one side as if the wires were a bit slack.

Do you know that funny moment when you're mad in a rage and you bash out at someone and it all goes funny before your eyes and you think you're going blind? The old brain seems to shift and twist and you can't see what you're looking at? Well, I suppose everyone knows what I mean; everyone gets mad.

I hit him then. Properly. Several times, it was. Maybe a few dozen good hits. I didn't forget to get his money, but he had no watch. I had to wipe my hands on his coat and at the finish there was so much blood and slobber everywhere I had to take out my thing to wash it off my hands and down the gutter. I hosed him down a bit, too, part out of spite, I reckon, and part to tidy his face up a bit so anyone who passed by would only think he was a drunk gone to sleep and leave him alone. I suppose it was anti-social, but your family has to come before the filthy public.

Bee got a bit extra that week to buy fruit for the kids. I told her to get herself a haircut out of the rest, she was always pushing this goldy colour hair out of her eyes. But that wasn't right away; after I'd rolled my first drunk I got back to the Zoo.

All round Sydney lights were on, all the people were sitting up in millions of houses filling in insurance policies on their fowls, their wrought-iron railings, concrete paths, light globes, their health, funeral expenses, borers, carpets, insuring against loss of work, loss of clothes, loss of conjugal rights, loss of money, loss of friends. I wonder if they had policies that could protect them from me.

I kept on like that for a few days, getting a bit here and there, quite a bit in fact, but something happened in the Zoo that got me kicked out. They didn't actually kick me out, but if they caught me they would have.

These people were looking round the Zoo, at the animals, making happy noises and plenty of litter with milk cartons, soft drink cans, lolly papers, sandwich crusts, and there was a kid there younger than me, about fourteen I'd say, a girl, with darker hair than Bee's and boy, was she pretty. She was that dark sort that has to shave their legs a lot later and right then the hairs on her legs were starting to grow, she was about that age, but I didn't worry too much about that, she had these beautiful red cheeks on her face. Apple-cheeks.

I couldn't help following them just to get a bit of a look at her now and then. You don't have to worry, they didn't notice me. But it got too much for me, and ever since I'd taught myself to roll a drunk I'd got more impulsive, if you understand me, and what did I do but buy a little bag of fruit and go up to her when she was a bit away from the others and give them to her. Or tried to, rather. I think I was even pleased that she said no thank you, that showed she wasn't too cheap and likely to say yes to anyone. But I felt a fool having to eat the whole bag myself—a bag of apples—so I asked her again then sort of put them in her hands. She had brown eyes that the sun got into, the sun sort of got under the brown and shone them up very shiny.

Well, they got too wide to be pretty. She started making loud screams and a lot of people took out after me. In twenty minutes everything was quiet again, I'd lost the chasers and the girl was looking in at the snake cages where the poor old snakes were having a snooze since their cages faced the sun. She even forgot the apples enough to start tapping the glass cages to wake up the snakes. I watched her, a bit disgusted; she tapped every cage. But I couldn't forget those apple-cheeks. And until I left there I had the feeling I was being followed. Any minute I thought someone would come up behind me and say, 'This is the one that raped that girl in the Zoo.' I didn't rape her, you know I didn't, but everyone knows how these things get blown up when the public gets hold of them. They don't care what happens to the original facts, they don't even know if the original facts were facts.

I had to go; they were on to me and I didn't want to be shot out. I tell you what, I felt so good that no one could catch me—a sort of energy or power—that I ring-barked every tree in the park with my knife. There was a silly war statue there, too. I knocked the arms off that, they were the only things on it that I could twist. Boy, did they make a fuss about that! Don't they act up when you touch their property! Do people think their silly old property will ride proud and shiny before them into heaven?

I had felt quite at home in the Zoo. The peacock was one of my favourites. He'd lift his tail up to impress you and there'd be staring eyes all over it, looking through you. Come to think of it, I felt quite at home in the whole world, doing what came into my head. But I must admit that sometimes I almost stopped to wonder who put all these things in my head in the first place. I used to laugh at the animals and tell them they were in hell. Get it? They'd been bad in Africa or South America or where they came from, so they were sent here to hell in cages. They were just the bad ones. And when I left the Zoo I remember thinking it's just the same for people. Or maybe it's just the same. This is hell now, the after-life we were sent to because we were bad where we came from. That's why practically everyone you know has such a lot of bad in them.

It seemed a good idea when I first had it, but I soon got tired of it. I get sick of everything very quickly.

2
CAVE

I walked all the way back to this cave I knew, seventeen miles from midnight to five o'clock. The darkness was warm. It was when I was near streetlights or shopfront lights that I felt the cold. I lay back and had a rest till the sun was up a bit. I thought of myself lawless as a meteor, burning what I touched.

The cave, if you lay back and looked out of it, was nothing more than a hole in the rock, aimed one way at the cooling core of this poor old dying planet, and the other way at a big sweep of outer nothing. Before I got round to getting something to eat, I started to scratch some drawings inside the roof of the cave with the pig-stabber end of my knife. It was a high cave and I had to get some thick saplings stuck in side ledges to reach up there. I cut fairly deep into the sandstone, then rubbed in some dirt and ashes from the floor. They were pretty coarse drawings. I got rid of the saplings and dusted off the marks they made.

I thought I heard a footslip noise outside. When I edged my head round to look there was nothing, only maybe a peewit had rattled a stone loose somewhere. But something saw me. The first I heard was a drumming on the soft ground, a rabbit bobbed away uphill. I chased him till he squatted, crept up on him, he started away in a big circle, then ended up near the cave again, where he went to ground. I used some of his scrape to block up his holes, then dug him out from his main entrance. Rabbits have to die alone, their mates clear out when there's trouble.

I stretched him, headed him, skinned him, gutted him, chopped off his hands and feet and had him for breakfast. There's nothing like meat in the morning.

And there's nothing like the great sound of things breaking, splintering, crashing and smashing. With the meat in me I hurled big stones down and toppled three mighty rocks from the top of the hill; you should have seen them go bashing down through the trees, knocking everything flat bash to the creek. The grass and flowers moved and shook so much you'd think they were laughing, too.

I reckon any of the ordinary people who could have seen me then would have wanted to be me. But it was a weekday and they turn into workers on weekdays, not humans any more. They're bricklayers, accountants, truck drivers, doctors, coppers. Humans on weekends.

Now and then I had trouble sleeping there in the cave. I must have had it on my mind about someone following me. Things were always running around in my head one after the other, chasing one another. Even the things in my head had other things following them! That made me laugh.

I hate to be a member of anything. Member. It's a cow of a word. It's all right visiting people, looking in on them, but the word membership...Come to that, all those words with ship on the end give me a pain; friendship, membership, kinship, relationship.

Stealing, stealing...That was all I ever did, practically. Just a matter of taking what you want when you like. Stealing other people's friends, stealing money, food, even stealing a bit of shelter from those who didn't miss it.

One bad day a year ago I spilled bath water on little Stevo's leg. We had to heat up the water in the copper and carry it up the steps, fourteen steps—I made them myself out of fenceposts from the bush; the holes that used to carry the eight-gauge wire made good drainholes—you carried the water up the steps and poured it into the bath, but if someone was in the way or mucking about near the edge of the bath they could easily get a gallon of boiling water over them. Stevo did. I knew I could have stopped it splashing him if I'd wanted to. Why did I want to hurt him? Was it because when they were really hurt they ran to Bee?

You know, there was a spoon in our family right from the time I was very young up to the present day. It was worn thin and it was mainly used for the castor oil Ma used to drop into the kids, but I liked that spoon. Funny, how you can like a thing that's got no life in it, when you don't like most of the things that do have life. Remember, I'm only telling you these things because you want to know.

When we moved into the old place in Short Street some kids had shot rocks all over the floor in every room in the house. The old man didn't say much, I reckon he'd done his share of shotting rocks, but poor old Ma was the one that had to clean up the mess. My cousin Jim, the one that was in some place called Changi many years ago, used to visit us. I remember him riding his motorbike full bore up the hill to Chiswick, and taking me to the Art Gallery. He was an artist and drew pictures to decorate the officers' tents in the war—you know, naked women—he even studied later at the Julian Ashton Art School, but we gave those Gallery attendants a few good afternoons. They really earned their money keeping on our tracks.

They must have had some rule about people not touching the paintings, because if you let your finger stray too close to the paint, the attendants would start walking towards you very fast. And if you took your finger away, they would stop where they were and pretend to turn away. I suppose the point was, if you weren't dressed very well and you were young, they got worried. Course, if you put your finger out again and again, they would keep stopping and starting. Worry makes them very nervous.

The old man used to try to sell fish then, that was after the old brethren disapproved of his good insurance job. He didn't like it either, then, what with most of the people having to surrender their policies, he thought it was cruelty, but he could have said to hell with the brethren, couldn't he? Did we mean less to him than his principles? I reckon we did. But I'm not sore about it any more, it's no use anyway, he's dead and buried.

23

There was the bomb shelter I dug in the backyard. I ought to fill it in, you can't expect Stevo to know the difference between a red-back and a blow-fly. You asked me to tell you what I remember, didn't you?

I shouldn't have bashed that porcupine to death. Not with my tommyhawk. Not with anything. I could have dug him out and given him to Stevo as a pet.

Why did they? Why me? Of all the people I could have been, why did I come out as me? I could have been anybody. It must have been the way they did it, the wrong time or the wrong way or something. When Ma was expecting me, she walked along George Street and was just in time to see a couple of coppers belting the shine off the old man for loitering. Actually he was waiting for her. And me. He must have talked back and you can't do that unless you've got some standing in the community. And before I came she saw one day at the foot of Napoleon Street a mass of loyal workers, showing solidarity through the boot, kicking a scab to death. Maybe those little episodes soured me right from the time I was an egg.

I called in at the house just on dark. Stevo was about to be got ready for bed. I waited around while Bee tucked the others in.

'When you taking us to Wisem Beddy?' said Stevo. He meant Wiseman's Ferry. I'd forgotten I'd promised.

'See? I say Wisem Beddy.' Bee must have been trying to correct him. 'Boots says it.' Boots was some character on the TV. I got them a set off one of those delivery trucks that double park while the driver hefts into the appliance shops the cartons of new stuff from the manufacturers. It's simple. You wear ordinary clothes as if you're offsiding on the truck, then hit the goods as soon as the driver's on the footpath with his load. You carry your own load towards a shop then go down a lane or through a shop out the back. If you watch the delivery routes and only hit the manufacturers' trucks you can't go wrong. I don't believe in knocking off the owner-drivers. They're on their own, like me. It wasn't a big set.

'Time to go sleepy-byes,' said Bee, a bit severely.

'I wouldn't not like no seepy-byes,' said Stevo. 'Want to stay and watch the snow-pens.' That was the penguins. They were on the TV too. Practically everything was on TV. If you had enough money, you could almost kid yourself you were living, by watching the thing all the time it was on.

'Get your night suit, then I'll give you your bath.'

'You hab a bath, if you want to.' But she swung him off his feet and headed for the bathroom.

'Would you like to get his night suit. Under his pillow,' she called back to me. I knew she must be tired, it wasn't like her to ask for help. I got it, anyway, although I don't like doing things for people. I went in the bathroom and shot the pyjamas over the towel-rack. It squeaked a bit in its brackets, it must have been getting rusty.

'Don't do that! Mustn't! I told you!' Stevo ordered. 'That not the place!' Bee must have told him to put certain things in certain places. I didn't see any difference, myself. I was about to put the pyjamas somewhere else, when Bee whipped them off the rack and shot them on to a little sort of table. I reckon she had those certain troubles. I've noticed that the ones that are anxious about men or the future are the ones that have the most trouble. And of course you only suffer like that with nerves if you don't take the things you want right away, when you want them. That's what I always do. I have no anxiety, that I know of. It's the only way. She probably thought to herself that I was a problem kid from a good girl's point of view, who falls in love immediately and forgets absolutely the next moment. Mind you, I don't know if that's what she thought, but if she did, she was right.

Anyway, Stevo was in the bath and looking for some way to stay out of bed. I thought I'd get out of the road before he started on his Chantic Bird. It was probably only a kid's fairy story and didn't mean a thing. He could see I was going to vanish, and the way he looked at me wasn't quite the same as when the bathwater hit his leg. I was glad of that.

I always get to my hidey-holes as quiet as I can, and when I got back to the cave and crept round the entrance, the sound of the cave's inside wasn't the same as before. That was my first idea there was someone there. It wasn't as echoey. Not as hollow. I was always a bit worried that someone might be wanting to latch onto me and tag along behind. A sort of side-kick. But I'm no good with someone else. I have to do things my own way, I don't even like anyone watching.

Then I heard whiskers. The sound of a hand rubbing upwards the short bristles at the back of a head. The sort of head that gets a short back and sides. A man, most likely.

When he clicked his torch on I could see it was, too. Apart from his short haircut he was an arty sort of joker. And what was he doing? He was trying to follow the aboriginal cave drawings he'd discovered on the ceiling of the cave. He couldn't reach them, but there he was, copying them down in a book. I bet he never saw cave drawings like that before. Made by ten-foot high aborigines. Then I startled myself a bit. He moved his old torch a fraction and it seemed someone black slid around the cave wall at me. It was only shadows, though. When he had the torch unsteady you'd swear there was a crowd of people up the back of the cave.

He was a nuisance. Odds on he had no money with him. As I walked away very quietly I cursed him and wished he had a job. At least a job would have kept him out of my way. That's what jobs are for, to keep people off the streets.

3
BUSH

I didn't sleep long enough to want to bounce up fresh as soon as I woke, I was camped out in the bush, but when I did get around to having a wash in the creek—it was the start of the Lane Cove where I was—I had to climb up into the trees, the morning felt so good. I sprang a bit from branch to branch, actually I called it flying but I don't think I was anywhere near as pretty as the glider possums that do that sort of thing all the time. Naturally I had to fall. Only about eight feet, though, onto what we used to call Indian Rock, since from the side it had a hook nose and a fierce face. Where I hit, a paper-thin layer of stone whispered up loose from the rock. I crumbled it into the sand it was and started to feel my leg. There was a bit of a rip just above the knee. I got some cold water on it and stopped the blood. I knew my way about cuts like those. A few miles away, some jets dived and climbed, then raced peacefully high up, leading a white vapour trail back to base.

I wandered about through the bush, had a good drink at old Roach's pool—old Roach, I knocked down my first pedestrian outside his house on the footpath; it was a little kid and I was on a pushbike and he got me a mention in the local rag—listening to the crickets in the grass and the little waterfalls in the creeks. If I'd had some meat I could have had some crayfish for dinner if I'd had some string to tie the meat to.

I lifted the bark of a young red gum and did a little drawing with my knife on the wood of the tree. The cambium layer, they called it in school. I put back the bark, hoping it wouldn't die, and went away hoping someone would get a surprise if they were passing by when the bark peeled around November. When I thought about it later, I had to admit there wasn't much chance anyone would pass by just at that time, but there was something like a shadow of a chance.

I felt like some fruit, so I crossed the rusty railway lines and trotted through the bush to Dural. There was plenty of fruit there, always. On the way I remember thinking it was the same bush I walked in when the old man tried to tell me the facts of life. Someone put him up to it, because he didn't want to. I could see that. Mostly it was because he didn't really take to me, I didn't look like his side of the family, in fact I was dark and reminded him of Ma. He liked the ones with fairer colour and blue eyes.

It was in that bush that I got flowers years ago and pressed them in a botany book and got special commendation, whatever that was. Actually, it meant nothing; they often used to give a prize a big name if there wasn't actually any value in it.

I went by the little old house where a dog came at me once so fast that he left a bruise, a ten-inch bruise on my leg for months. He was running so fast I thought he was going on past. The collision must have dazed him a little for he just stood there and shook his head. I grabbed it, the head, with my hands over his mouth to clamp his jaws shut, put my legs round him, then sat on his back and rolled over. That had him in a neat scissors. You have to watch out for their paws even if their claws are blunt. The scissors was around his waist and all I had to do then was bend him back; usually their backs break. This one was a bit whippy in the spine, so I had to choke him. I threw it on the front verandah of the little house. It was one of those old houses with a lot of bushes around the front door, like so much fur. I thought it was pretty suggestive, but that might have been my lewd imaginings, like the censorship says.

A few hundred yards away from the house is the ti-tree bush, we called it tick-bush, the very bush where a kid called Willie started his family. Just before he got married. A few times I broke a bit of that bush off and stuck it in his front door; it was a laugh for a while, but I got sick of that too.

I had a shirt full of fruit, then I got the idea of digging out a rabbit and having a feast. I planted the fruit, started a bunny, chased it to its burrow, blocked up the escape holes and dug through from the main entrance. I got to his legs and tried to pull him out, but he was halfway round a corner, so I broke his back legs and dug down to him. I think he would have bitten me if he could, but I stretched him.

The next thing was something to drink. There was a church nearby, not more than a mile away, so I got in there and the place I got in was some kind of room where the minister had his office. The churches where they don't have much space, all you look for is a store-room; if there is no store-room, you look for a divan with frilling down the sides to hide what's underneath. I got a whole case of altar wine there. Not a bottle missing, and that's handy when you have to carry it; there's no rattles. I got it out a side door and over the fence.

I stayed there in the bush near the orchard about three days, until the wine was gone. The first night went quick; in no time at all the sky disappeared star by star and nothing but a blank glare was left. There was light everywhere.

I remember making myself a mattress of branches; I slaughtered a few small trees by breaking off their tops, and arranging them in a sort of trench that kept the wind off me, and I remember a few of the things that went through my head.

Naturally there was the old one that always kept coming back: something's going to happen to me. With a skinful of wine I could afford to treat this one lightly. And there was the sound of rain on corrugated iron. Ever since I was young I remember listening to the rain on our tin roof, it was a good feeling to pull the sheet and the blanket over your head and let your breath warm you up and all the time the rain pelting down, roaring onto the rusty roof, and you there snug, knowing it was that piercing sort of cold, rain-cold, outside.

Old McCarthy spun round in my head, too. I laughed out loud when I remembered my old man telling me that mister Mac would kill himself carrying home those huge big logs on his shoulder. Because the old man died shortly after and old Mac went for years, and didn't die before he was fifty, like my old man; he lived to be eighty. And he died running for a train.

I was a bit sad that the old bunch of kids had broken up. We used to have these wars down the bush, you weren't supposed to shoot to kill, just to aim near the enemy. Matter of fact, we made a rule to get a few hundred yards away so the bullets would have lost most of their punch if they hit. Just the same, there were always the smart ones that wanted to creep up. It made me pretty mad, because I never crept up on the others. I hate anything like that. I mean if I'd done it too, they probably wouldn't have lasted beyond the first battle. They knew I could creep so no one could hear, I reckon they just relied on my good nature. Anyway, I was mad. I always regretted it later, but I shot one of the kids. The docs couldn't take the lead out because it was too near his heart. He still carries it round in his chest.

What with feeling sad for the old days, after I finished the altar wine and the fruit and the rabbit, I got a bit lonely, something I don't often do. I went back to the house and asked Bee to fix my leg. She got me to sit on the table and put my foot, shoe and all, on her clean lap. But what got me, when she saw the gash, she gave a sort

32

of gasp and looked worried. I was surprised, of course, but I was pleased too, in a way. It was like congratulations, to have her worried about me. The skin of her fingers was soft, and only about as warm as flowers growing in the sun.

Sitting there like that reminded me of Ma and the times she fixed up my cuts when I was a kid, and along with her I thought of her Marie Stopes book that I used to read when I felt a bit down. Boy, what an artificial life my parents must have had. I used to laugh about that book, but I don't think they did. Maybe they knew what they were doing when they had all of us, but I don't think so.

Stevo had his old Christmas cards out again. He used to keep whole piles of them from one year to the next. I leaned over his shoulder and read some for him and when he was slow turning them over I flicked over a few myself. But he knew what he wanted. He picked out a bundle and handed them to me. 'You hab a read,' he said. I was too fast for him. He went back to turning them over at his own pace. I liked that. He didn't hesitate to rubbish me when I was wrong.

He soon had an attack from another front. Allie was making for his cards.

'Why are you blocking Bubby's way?' asked Bee.

'Bubby going to make a 'stake,' he said. Allie was not easy to turn back.

'I'll ring up the police…Indians will come…' Stevo didn't know what to say to impress her. 'There'll be tigers in the bush.' But he had to give up. Nothing stopped Allie.

Bee said to me, so Stevo could hear, 'Elaine tells me the twins came home from Sunday school and said that God makes rain.' That got to Stevo.

'We don't want any talk like that here.' He had strong ideas on rain, ever since Bee tried to tell him about the sun and the clouds.

'Turn the light off!' he ordered me. 'It's wastefou!' He was on the ball all right, I'd forgotten I flipped the switch. I wasn't used to being ordered about, though. It reminded me of the kids' games we used to play with the girl next door before her parents got her to play with some nicer friends.

Bee told me Stevo had added some fantastic bits to his story of the Chantic Bird, ready to tell me. But just then, he wanted to go out and play with Chris in the pile of sand I got for them from the council job up the street. She fed me a cup of tea and some dry biscuits with tomato and salt, but I went before Stevo got back.

I don't know if you like being in the bush at night, but I do. There's something pretty good in coming out of a place that's dark and secret and leaving your mark on the people that hate the dark, then going back where they can't follow you. I used to come out at night to fill in the trenches that the council dug in the daytime. Whenever I needed a few hours' good slogging I'd take a spade from someone's back-yard and raise a sweat pushing dirt back in holes. There were always plenty of council holes. I bet they scratched their heads in the mornings. I think Bee had a good idea it was me; I bet she thought I was crazy. You couldn't have got me to dig a hole in anyone's garden, unless it was to bury something, or to look for treasure with Stevo.

A worker came by while I was filling in. Practically everyone you see is a worker. Maybe he had been laying for me. Up to then the only company I had was an owl going by, giving the air soft thumps with his wings.

'Say, son,' he opened his speech. Son always impresses me.

'Son, we're trying to get the ruddy council finished here. They've been digging in our street for weeks. What you're doing will only prolong their mess.' I made my usual signs that I was deaf and pretty soon he went away. They always do. I liked to think it was my face helped me, and my sincere manner, but it was probably only the spade, which was pretty sharp and flashed cheerfully in the light from the nearest light-pole.

I got another interested visitor. A kid from one of the local gangs fancied himself as a spotter and tried to creep up on me while I was digging. I slipped into the trench and got round behind him. I felt vicious enough to backhand him from here to Stockinbingal and back. My chest had that relaxed feeling.

You can't be hurt when you're bashing at something. When you shot a kero tin in the air and punch it coming down, you call an extra toughness out of the air. I only hit him a few times, then I gave it away for the night. I tossed the spade over the nearest fence and off. They can keep their gangs, I won't be regimented. There's no freedom doing what someone else decides.

I used to have a little trick that impressed the neighbours when I got wood for the old man. I'd take the old Kelly axe and trim up one of the coachwood trees, at least that's what I called them. A thirty-foot log about a foot through was light as a feather when it was nice and dry. The inside of it smelled like a perfume and the grain wavy and shiny.

As I went back into the bush to sleep, all sorts of things came up to the surface of my mind, things I thought I'd forgotten. The dead cat in the bush pool, all white and skinned. The first time I ever thought how lonely it was to die away somewhere where no one could bury you... And my mother dying, with my sister crying and yelling; she thought I was a ghoul for wanting to hold Ma's hand while she went.

'Do you want to hear the very last breath?' she yelled at me. Yes, I did. But you couldn't answer someone in that state. Ma was in a coma, but you never know, she might have had a little flash before that last breath, and she might have been glad there was someone to hold her hand steady.

I was an early bird once. There was a Jubilee or something when I was a kid and all our class got dressed up in pink galah outfits. Pink and grey. All except me and another kid, we were too poor to afford the costumes, so we minded the bags and lunches. We were the only ones to eat our lunches, we ate them straight away, while the others were in the showground. When they got back, everything had melted and all their sandwich fillings run. It was a very hot day.

You sure you want all these things I remember? OK, but don't blame me for the way they look.

Bee told me that one of her friends reckoned I was the one that used to take Missus Major to the vacant block and fill her with brown muscat, but it wasn't me. I never went near her, it was big Mac.

I still can't forget chasing that turkey round the house at Rosehill. Or was it a duck? I think it was a turkey. When you've chased something and you're just about to clobber it, you get a moister feeling in your mouth. Did you ever notice it? It must have been a turkey. I hit old Roy's kid with a stone once, he was a cheeky kid, and old Roy came down the bush after me with the rest of them. I ended up chasing them home with rocks. I wish I could throw a rock now like I could then, when I was young.

I got back to my little spot of shelter and pulled my blanket of branches over me and while I dropped off to sleep there was this sentence I heard going round in my head, from the woman next door. 'Why doesn't he get drunk—like a man?' I couldn't make out if it was about me or not. She didn't realise it was dangerous to get drunk, it depended where you did it. Some of the fellows I know, you don't want to get drunk near them. They'd bottle you for two bob if they thought you were half shot.

Next day I nearly killed a swaggie. Round near Name cave he was sleeping, and unluckily for him I was thinking of a pig I killed once and how when it was on its side, dead, it gave a kick and opened my leg to the bone, and I was feeling so mad with that pig that I almost picked up a rock and smashed the swaggie's head in. For a moment I got him mixed up with that pig. I don't know what stopped me, but I couldn't help smiling to see him sleeping so near a track. His mouth was open, like an old man's—he was an old man—and flies were round it and in it too.

This memory of mine is a funny thing; I couldn't tell you what I had for tea last night, but if someone looked at me sideways ten years ago, I'd remember that. I had nothing much to do then, so when I saw a brown snake I chased it. Brown snakes can certainly move, did you ever chase one? Well, after about forty yards it was hard to tell who was doing the chasing. All of a sudden it went to ground under a tuft of grass and I knew it must have been me that chased it.

I got to thinking about all the things I remembered, sitting on a favourite rock of mine above Lorna Pass, and I must have gone to sleep. I had another coloured dream. I was being chased along this narrow track in the bush, it must have been at the bottom of a valley, 'cause there were fallen logs across the track and it was very cool and the air felt wet. The colours of the dream were green and brown and I fell down on the ground and the man chasing me had a rifle and I crouched on the damp earth for a spell while he took aim and put a bullet through my head. The funny thing was, I felt the bullet go in. I woke up, feeling very cold, yet I was wet with sweat. Green and brown, and I can't remember who shot me.

I got out of there but it wasn't my day. When I got near the spot where I shot the pups, I just forgot to watch where I put my feet. The next thing, I trod right on where I'd buried them. There was movement under my foot and looking down I saw the maggots. And a patch of damp brown fur.

I walked with more care after that, even though I'd passed the only spot where I'd buried anything, and I suppose the pups and the dream and the snake and the swaggie with the flies were all on my mind, 'cause next thing I found I was talking to myself.

'I know I didn't visit the old man until it was too late, but neither did you. Any of you.' The people I was talking to weren't exactly there, yet in a way they were.

I stopped for a drink at Roach's pool. The water comes down through the veins of the hill and bleeds into the little old space behind the patted cement retaining wall, just enough to give you a good drink. On all sides the ground sloped down to the pool, with a rock track down on one side through the sandstone walls of the gully. It was an ideal place to set a trap for someone. Maybe, a hundred years ago, some settler with the pioneering spirit baited some steak with arsenic so the blackfellows would get the idea they weren't wanted. Come to that, you could have shot them, in safety, as they had a drink at the pool. As I bent down to drink like a lizard I felt strangely vulnerable. When I got up to the main track on the flat at the top of the hill I thought I saw the ranger. Not old Roach; he's dead. Then I knew those other things, the dream, the snakes and all, were a warning; he'd been tracking me. I didn't want him to see my face, so I ran. So did he, but I lost him easily. I hope he didn't see my face. If he did, he'd better not pester Bee and the kids; I get very protective about those kids. When I think of them.

4
CEMETERY

You won't want to know me when you hear this chapter. I was living in the cemetery at the time, but all I'd had for a day or two was potatoes, so I sneaked back to Bee's house. If you're quiet enough, you can get in anywhere, people always have their doors open in the daytime; everyone seems to think there's something about the daylight that's more innocent than the dark. Don't believe them.

Anyway, I was in the ceiling having a bit of a listen to the littlies getting used to being alive, waiting for a few hours to pass so I could turn up in time for dinner. Nothing more than that, I wouldn't hurt Bee. Those kids were characters.

Don't get me wrong; you can get a good feed any time you like, any place. But it was fun listening to Stevo, he and Chris were actually practising talking, and laughing to each other. Now and then there'd be a yell and Bee's voice would appear on the sound track.

'Who did that?' she'd say.

'Sum buddy,' Stevo would answer and both would laugh. When Chris trod on his hand, he said gallantly, 'My hand won't hurt, Mum. I eat pickles.' Food made strength straightaway for Stevo.

I could see him transferring Bee's brown sugar from the basin to the lid. From the lid it went you know where. If he was caught, he'd say he was cleaning the lid. After a bit, he said, 'I'm a little bit upset, Mummy.'

'Why are you a little bit upset?'

''Cause I want to be a little bit upset.' He just wasn't game to own up.

The usual thing happened and he wet his pants. He got the stick for that.

'Just a little stick,' said Bee with a coaxing voice.

'Lilly stick!' he yelled as she hit his legs, and he hopped about, crying a bit.

'Lift me up, Mummy. You're a big girl now.' I could have listened all day.

When Bee took them out for the afternoon walk, she made sure the kids went to the toilet first. But Stevo had some idea of being equal.

'Mummy wee-wees, too.' She laughed. It was a nice sound.

I got down through the manhole while they were out, and when Bee got back to do the ironing, there I was. She was never surprised to see me. She told me, soon as she clapped eyes on me, that Stevo was pretty upset that

41

I walked out on him last time when he wanted to tell me his story. She said I should listen, because he looked up to me.

After being so close to Bee that I could have talked in a whisper and had her hear me, I just had to have a woman. Bee looked so good you could eat her. I bet if there was no religious prejudice against eating people there'd be a lot of killings. I've seen people with the sort of meat on them that you'd never find on a bullock or a smelly old sheep, although I think someone you liked would taste better than someone whose guts you hated. But that's no good, you'd only kill the ones you liked. I feel peculiar when I even think of hurting Bee, not that I don't think of it, but I couldn't do it. Couldn't. What I meant was what about all the famous lovers? They practically eat one another, what with kissing and slobbering and biting. To hear about them, you'd think there wasn't any part of your girl friend that you couldn't put on a plate with potato and peas.

Anyway, there I was back in the cemetery on the prowl. If you want to hear better and breathe quieter, the thing to do is open your mouth and breathe through it. You'd be surprised how many people have given themselves away with the sound of their breathing. And you'd be amazed if you knew how many times I've got away from someone simply by hearing them a few seconds before they heard me. I'm not exaggerating.

I've heard a person's eyelids click. And I thought I was caught once, but what I could have sworn was a man muttering as he was about to grab me, was only two trees rubbing.

When I went prowling I often thickened up my eyebrows, wore a few extra clothes in case I had to shed some to get away, or else wore a leather jacket. You'd be surprised how frightened people are of a leather jacket. Kids dressed in leather get the blame for all sorts of things.

Mind you, I only had a go at the sheilas that needed a bit of excitement. Except when the young ones looked too good to miss. The one I got that day in the cemetery wasn't too good-looking, in fact some people might say she was a bag. She was short and a bit wide. You'd call her a thick girl. You felt her thighs were rubbing together under the dress material.

She was one of those that can wreck a pair of shoes in one day; you know, they're all over on one side with foot spilling everywhere and toes and heels roughed up. But she was a girl. Under her stringy hair, which was a sort of beige colour, she had this round face which was much the same colour. Come to think of it, her dress was beige, too.

Her legs were prickly where she had shaved, and I'd say she had about four days' growth of stubble. Still, she was a girl. She didn't have to shave her face, and that was a relief. She reminded me of a girl called Jean I knew when I was in Russell Lea kindergarten. Every afternoon we used to chew up wheat grains and make a sort of chewy mixture. It was great fun. Every afternoon for a week or two, I mean. I must have been one then, or five; some age like that.

She didn't yell much. She was probably used to being attacked in the cemetery, lots of people hang around Rookwood. She even tried to kiss me. I didn't like that because she had food around her teeth, where the teeth go into the gums, and as I sort of turned away, my elbow caught her on the side of the chops, and she got upset and lay face down, having a bit of a sob.

So just to round off what I actually meant to be a sexual attack, I got out my runny old Biro and wrote on her backside, 'Neglected, exposed to moral danger'. She asked me what the words were and I said, 'I love you'. The words didn't come out too clearly because I hate saying 'love' and I always say it pretty softly, but she didn't seem to doubt me. If she had asked me why there were more letters than you need to write I love you, I was going to say I went over the letters a couple of times, but she didn't ask me. Two beetles on the ground joined up end to end, looking in opposite directions. Doing it because something inside commanded them. I tried not to think of my own parents.

There was another girl I saw later, she reminded me of a girl called Rene that I used to give rides on my pushbike when I was much younger, about eleven, and I was just about to slide out from behind someone's big flat slab and race up behind her, lift and gag her in one move and keep going for the grass on the other side of the road, when I heard the clatter of a car on the loose board of one of the bridges over the culverts. I took that as a sign of danger and let her go. Some days I get very superstitious.

When you grab a girl like the beige girl, you're not really attacking her. Not even molesting. If you were, you'd soon see headlines in all the papers. The trouble with the kids that end up in court is, they ditch the girl as soon as they get satisfaction and generally treat her like a bit of dirt. If they took the trouble to take her out somewhere and let her down easy, they'd be free. Unless you get a real hard case girl that's been brought up wrong with a chip on her shoulder against men. Then you're in strife, and you may have to finish her off.

I played a joke on the cemetery keeper, or whatever they call him. The one that goes round just to see everything is falling to pieces at the right rate. There'd been a cave-in in one of the crypts, the kind where rich people get buried. Someone had been in there, young kids probably, and opened the newest coffin. All I did was move the coffin near the entrance, and took out the old girl inside it and propped her up where you'd see her if you were checking up on cave-ins. She looked like the old landlady we had, I used to have to go up and give her the rent; Ma wouldn't go, she said the landlady gave her the creeps, what with being so old and looking dead till you said, 'Hem', in your throat.

'Live and let live,' she'd say. The landlady. Anyway, this cadaver was sitting up; I spread her arms and took the cloth off her. I was surprised there wasn't more of a smell, but her appearance was frightful. I had to get a fair way away from the crypt to watch, I even had to leave a trail of bottles and papers to draw the man's attention to my little trick, but it was worth it. You should have seen that man go to water when he clapped eyes on the poor old lady corpse propped up there starkers.

Of all people, why did I turn out to be me? Now and again I get the miserables, I can't help it. I was leaning up against a tall flat slab with a round point at the top, and a spot on the right side of my head, above the ear, rubbed on the slab edge. At the same time I got a funny tickle on the right side of my neck, at the back. I did it some more, and got the same tickle. I thought about it for a bit, then I felt so sleepy I went straight to sleep in the sun, between two old granite blocks.

They were all done up in a lot of clothes and smarmed with greases and powders as if their fine ageing bodies held a great mystery and must be preserved. I stood on the edge of the crowd round the hole in the ground that the men in the yellow digging machine had made the day before. They were singing songs I didn't know, but I joined in with bits of songs I had picked up from juke boxes and top of the pops parades. I couldn't actually say I know one song right through. Not one. Only the very old ones my auntie Olive used to sing when I was a very young kid. And you never hear them now. So there I was, leaning backwards against a thin whitish stone and mumbling the words that came into my head, like 'Shake it, baby, pretty-eyed baby, you're the neatest one, paper-doll baby, let's move, you hear me, let's move it, c'mawn baby, get me outa here…' And so on. I didn't mean anything by it, except I'd never sung at a funeral before, not even my brother's, or Ma's, or the old man's. It didn't seem the right thing to do. Just shutting up would have been better. Silence. While they put on their clay blanket. And the funeral car men fidgeting around their cars, dying to get away, and trying to have a smoke without anyone seeing.

Anyway, this slab I was leaning against broke. That put me down on top of a vegemite jar of plastic flowers. I was still riding the slab so I didn't cut myself when the jar broke, although I did have time to hear the nice sound of the breaking glass. And they chased me. Right in the middle of the singing, with the box still topside. The whole lot of them, except a couple of thick old ladies. I think the average person has a lot of savagery in him, far more than you'd think to see him standing with no hat on looking at the ground, making no comment and listening to the sound of some tired old minister mooning on and on, lie after lie. You couldn't help agreeing if you'd seen those mourners chase me. The car drivers didn't move. They took their cigarettes out from behind their backs and smoked openly.

Mourners have more speed than you'd think. By the way, if you don't think it's fair what I said about the lies, you listen at your next funeral. It's the ministers' fault. No one is as good as they say; no one is an inspiration for good; no one is a kind, good, generous, loving person. At odd times a few are, but the way they put it you'd assume they were like that all the time. People are just people; dirty and clean, good and mean, generous and dishonest. Actually the average person is pretty rotten, if you ask me.

I got away, but some of the young ones nearly caught me. They'd had no exercise all day, what with standing around waiting, so they were fresh. I ran into the shade in a culvert and got my breath back in the cool. I laughed a bit about the slab, I can still hear the thick crack of it, and the sort of shrieky laugh of the glass.

It's not much fun singing in the street, but if you keep saying to yourself that the listeners are rubbish, you can do it easily enough. I tidied my clothes, specially around the neck—people like you to be neat around the collar and wet my hair with some beer and sang a few songs outside a pub not far from the cemetery. This got me enough for a good meal and a couple of schooners of beer. I can get served in a pub because I'm sort of big for my age. Funny thing, to get served in a pub I have to ruffle my collar and mess up the old hair.

I didn't feel cold that night. I walked about a bit on the cemetery roads thinking of things like you do when you've had a few beers and nowhere special to go, about Ma being dead and the optician still sending cards asking her to come and get her eyes tested, and the kids I used to play with and fight with, some of them are respectable now with jobs and higher purchase, but they look old. And how when the old man was lowered away, his brother, my uncle, that broke his nose with a brass candlestick, had tears in his eyes, which I thought was a fine thing, and how the other uncle gave me an old watch he had no use for, but he was a Brother and wouldn't eat with us, not even a cup of tea...It wouldn't surprise me if they found parents and grown-up people to be the cause of kids like me and my naughty ways: they do the stupidest things, and try to make life complicated all the time.

I saw a funny thing over where the slabs end and the houses start. A man was waving a light to stop people going down a hole in the road, quite a few people come through the grounds after dark—the cemetery's a short cut to some places—but a man on a rusty bike thought it was someone like me up to tricks and swerved away. Naturally he went down the hole. It made me laugh, but I didn't stop thinking. I remembered my old man calling me in to his room, he had TB and had to have a room of his own, he asked me what I was going to do. He meant when I was older. I told him the first thing that came into my head, but when he said that it was getting dark up the street I knew something was wrong. A few mornings later Ma told me they were coming for him, so I tried to shave him with his own razor. I got a lot of stubble off but the parts near his chin were thick and strong and I left him with half a beard. They did a better job at Randwick. When he was dying and making a great racket in his throat I slept on the billiard table—I'd gone to visit him, it was only about the third time in three years—but in the morning he was dead, and they wouldn't let Ma see him.

Thinking about that reminded me of the girl I had when I turned sixteen. I must have made life hard for her, she had a small breakdown. It was plain enough to me that after a couple of days in hospital she'd be as good as a bought one, but why did she break down? What is it inside you that breaks? She was always nervy, very anxious to please everyone. Don't be like that. Don't be anxious to please everyone. Maybe she was pretending to have a breakdown.

Talking about breaking down, that was always a good trick in the cemetery. You get out of your car and wave to people when they come past, as if you're broken down. When they get out, you jump them. Easy. Another good trick was to put heaps of gunpowder out of bangers in the middle of the road, then light them in front of cars. Kids

I know bet on whether the driver will swerve or throw out the anchor. You should see the cars stand on their noses. If people went around prepared—ready for anything—as if they were in a jungle and the next minute might be their last they wouldn't get so het up about a simple little emergency.

Well, we fumigated the old man's room soon as he went. Then a couple of us had a room to sleep in instead of out on the verandah. I saw a picture of his grave once, there's another brother of mine takes more interest in these things than I do, but I didn't realise how miserable it was to be dead until I saw the grave when we buried Ma. You see, we put her on top of him in the one grave. Everyone said it was a nice thing and they'd want it that way, but actually it saved money. After all, we were paying for it.

That beer must have a loosening effect, because before I went to sleep I had to make a toilet out of a dirt grave. There was no stone or grave marker, so there was no harm done, only this slightly raised mound of dirt with strong—sharp and prickly—weeds growing on it.

That was a funny thought. The sharp grass, I mean. We were playing football on Woollahra oval one day and there were mounds and some digging outside the dressing rooms, which were in the stand. Mounds with sharp grass. It was a funny thought, because there in the cemetery it reminded me of two things. That day I saw a kid I hadn't seen since kindergarten in Russell Lea, a big tall kid who turned into a big tall man. Not all the big kids at school turned out big; some were much smaller than me, later. The other thing was, I saw that day a kid I hadn't seen since one day in old Jack Dunleavy's gym, a kid that came in and threw two hard rights into the heavy bag, then walked out. Later he was big-time, only he never turned pro. You actually get more glory when you stay amateur. I suppose it's just that the papers give more space to you. When I say you, or me, I mean him, of course; he got more glory. I won't, unless I do something spectacular. Or nasty. Which is easier.

When I stood up off the dirt grave, what should come into my head but the old neighbours we had and how quite a few of their sons never came back from the war. Some did, of course, but I reckon the best ones didn't, to hear their mothers talk.

When I awoke next morning I had the urge to draw something. I scouted round and found a cigarette packet, opened it out flat and drew on the inside a little drawing of that part of the cemetery. Just a sketch, with tombstones reaching into the distance and all sorts of funny monuments with wings and angels. What I did, I pushed it down a crack in a crypt to give the residents an idea of where they were.

I had a nasty experience there. It didn't start out nasty, but it got that way. It was a good day for a sunbake, so I stripped down to my underpants in a part of the cemetery that was very old and where no one came to visit. I put two bits of bark over my eyes because I don't like being blinded by the glare, and stretched out on my back. Bark is better than pennies, pennies get hot; and a handkerchief stops all of your face getting brown. Anyway, there I was, sunbaking on my back and when I got tired of that, on my stomach, which was really the most restful position. Now I'll tell you something you won't like; I was on a nice flat concrete grave, very old, but good and warm in the sun. And here's something else you won't like; I was letting the flies tickle me. Flies were pretty bad then and if you kept them off your eyes and mouth there was no harm in them. In fact, I like them. There were so many, it was like four girls, one blonde, one red, one black and one honey colour, drawing their fingernails softly over my skin. Their little fly feet had a kind of magic in them. Believe me, they're not as black as they're painted.

The reason the slab was warm, though, was that the earth had gone from under it. The blasted thing cracked under me, and I dropped down a bit over a foot. To cap it all, the headstone, one of those four-foot things, but thin in the old-fashioned style, fell inwards over me. Luckily it cracked at the base and I took some of the weight of it as soon as it started to fall. It was heavy as lead and tried to press me down into the grave and it took all I had to push it off me and get out of the hole. It frightened the flies away for a few seconds.

Then I noticed a man riding round and round on a bike. He had a sort of working uniform on, so I knew he was probably after me. It was time I wasn't there. I escaped, whistling, and do you know what I whistled?,

> When I was young and had no sense,
> I took a young girl behind the fence...

There was a fence round that oval where I took that young girl with the long brown hair. She didn't have apple-cheeks, she was pale and had a sort of long face, but boy, she had a big chest.

I often think to myself: Why did they do it and have me?

52

5
WHEAT SACKS

I get the feeling there's something waiting for me in the future. I don't know whether to say it will be good or bad and I daresay it doesn't matter, but it's more likely to be bad because good things don't often happen. I get no kick out of life, anyway.

As I vaulted the school fence—this was a long way from my cemetery—I remember I was humming to myself, Things were crook at Tallarook and there was no work at Bourke...I'm no expert, but I think that's a big part of our sprawly old country's history; things were crook. A truck boomed down a couple of gears round the corner and started to scream up the hill with its head down. The headlights were on high beam and they nearly blinded me. I can't stand brilliant lights when I'm in the dark. And I hate being illuminated.

There were plenty of times I wanted to wreck a school, but not because I had anything against them; I used to like school except for obedience. They used to give you points for doing what someone else said; I liked that about as much as a dog's bottom likes turps, and it affected me about the same. There was a wind in the wires that night; if anyone lit a school on a night like that all the fire brigades in Sydney couldn't stop it. Not that that says much.

Anyway, this wind whipping through the street wires covered me while I got inside. You know, all they ever tried to do was to teach us how to work for a boss, doing what you're told. And how to count his money and not do anything that would make him lose money. I suppose that sounds pretty all right to you; you're brought up to think that's the way things have to be. But they don't. All I have to do is get on my shoulderblades and look up at the sky and the clouds and I can think of lots of ways the world could be. But you wouldn't be interested, you couldn't go against what they taught you. And it wouldn't make you any happier.

I was in the part of the school where they teach the very young kids. There was a machine in the corner used for printing some of the guff they fed the kids. I looked at some of it and it wasn't as good as what they can get on TV, in the cartoons. Looking round the rooms, I felt a bit like I did when I lived next to Rosehill school, looking over the fence at a lot of kids racing round the sloping playground and wondering how it was there were so many other kids in the world. I gave the machine a belt; the silly things they were telling the kids took on a twisted shape like the metal I hit.

Now they might have to take the kids outside and show them the world, instead of kidding them you could put the world on paper with a pencil and sort of tame it, cut it up and move the bits around where you wanted, all on paper.

Some of the kids' drawings were on the walls. The boys drew clumsy trucks—I thought of when we went out into the country, we used to stand up in the back of the truck, shooting at anything that moved; you could find your way back home by the shine of brass cartridge cases—and both boys and girls drew animals. A blue picture of kittens switched my head back to when I used to have to drown bags of cats. The old man didn't like doing it and he didn't like giving them to me because he used to reckon I liked doing it; if you liked it, that was bad; the best thing was to hate it and do it without any fuss. Some crazy world. At my first job in a big factory, we had a telephone mechanic that used to hammer them. When we were one cat over, or if the cat we had did something he didn't like, he got out this great big hammer. The funniest thing was watching them run, after you clocked them. He used to be proud of his method and talk about it to the office girls, although he remembered to look sad and apologise for the poor pussy. If I had a hammer, I could have killed just as many as him, but he always made me beg him for the hammer.

My first kill was a long, thin tabby cat, with a high domed head. A natural target. I hit it fair and square between the ears, it dropped, spun round like a Catherine wheel, then got up. It charged across the room, hit the wall and charged back. It kept on doing this about six times and gave me time to swallow the extra spit that comes into

55

my mouth when I hit something that hasn't got a chance. Morgan hit it again, just to show I couldn't do it right, but it was dead on its feet. Anyway, there wasn't anyone else there to see if I'd done it wrong, but Morgan corrected me just the same. A lot of people are like that. I can't stand it. The stormwater drain was just outside; that's where we threw the cats. I almost made myself a promise to do the same for Morgan as I did for the cat, and see if he ran about after he was dead. But I wasn't sacked then, so I didn't feel so much against everyone.

I wrote a few things on the blackboard, because I knew they had girl teachers for the littlies, but then I looked round the room and saw in the light of the street globes the bits of drawings on the desks, and the nature table where the kids had their bottled snakes, the fish tank, and the rocks and birds' eggs, and up at the paintings the kids did and the remains of some careful writing where the teacher was showing them how to write, and it all looked so pathetic, as if they really wanted the kids to like going there, and so poor, as if the teachers knew there was no money for real decorations and bright things and got the kids to make their own—there was nothing on the floor, only the bare boards—honest, it was so harmless and well-meant that I couldn't do it. I thought of Stevo seeing what I was going to write and I got rid of the chalk. I nearly picked it up again when I saw a picture on the wall of a woman who didn't smile, but looked very confident. She looked clean, I won't say that, but it was the clean look of not ever having to do any work. She was the sort of sheila that took no trouble to make you like her. I took it down, smashed the glass carefully, and put her back on the wall. At least she could take the same chances as the kids' drawings and collect her share of flydirt and get dog-eared at the same rate as everything else.

I picked up a small pile of catty-looking rags the teacher must have used for wiping things and rubbed out my chalk words, then hung the rags like a tattered garland round the shoulders of the picture that I'd equalised. That's what I call it, equalising. Like death, lopping the lot to one size.

Out of the corner of my eye I caught a movement in a house about two hundred yards away. There was a bluish light in one window where the TV was, but the movement came near one of the dark windows. I gave up wrecking the school and climbed out of the window, keeping my eyes on the movement.

It was a kid. He'd got out of the window and closed it very slowly, with no noise. I got there, along the grass part of the footpath, just as he finished closing the window. I had to nip over a low fence to hide when he came towards me. He walked on the grass, too, pretty satisfied with himself and in no hurry. He had no coat on, so when I got to the house I took mine off. I knew there was a girl in bed in that room, maybe without a coat she'd mistake me for him. I did what he did, in reverse, but when I got in, she was fast asleep, so I got in the bed beside her and in her sleep she got used to the warmth of me. Probably she forgot he'd gone, or thought he'd come back, because for the next forty-five minutes my name was Greg. She was too lazy with sleep to do anything spectacular, but I got what I came for.

You had to laugh. The parents were inside watching a television programme while their daughter was being raped in her bed. I had one bad moment. Her wrist clicked and made a sound when there should have been no sound. Bear in mind, too, that I was taking a risk; they could have had any old disease for all I knew. You have to give me credit for that. Why, I could have been alive with crabs that same night. She hadn't bothered to have a shower before she let Greg in, but the chances are she'd be clean. The house looked neat enough, although you can't always tell from that.

Whoever set up this circus must be laughing. Whoever made a joker like me must have had funny moods. Here I am, wanting no one to be above anybody else, and yet I want to have nothing to do with the mob. Any mob.

I picked out a big pile of wheat sacks to camp in that night, in the yards of a flour mill. I thought I had a battle on my hands for one moment there. What might have been a watchman came through the yard at me, I thought he had a uniform, but he was only cutting through the yard to go to the car park, and it was only a pen pusher's uniform. Something flaps inside me when I'm about to clobber somebody. A wide, loose, flapping feeling in the bottom of my stomach, but only when I get angry.

The top of the pile was where I slept. I took out some of the middle sacks, built some walls round me down where it was warm, and pulled one over the top for a roof.

You know, I wouldn't like to get caught. They might cure me of doing what I like. If I could just live long enough

58

to give myself a chance to get tired of living. I wedged myself in amongst the bags and took a sight through my roof at the stars.

I was standing on something that didn't push back up with any pressure on my feet; I guess I was floating, standing up. The place was wide and dark, like a big lawn at night. There were fountains arching up and curving down, neon lights all colours shining in the water and in the mist floating away from the edge of the fountain jets and floating away up and over from the part of the stream where it loses height and breaks up, floating very cool down over the black skin of water shining with the colour you can't make out, smearing and running down the sides of tall glass buildings that caught with their edges and curves the full play of the lights of green and gold and blue and white and purple and amber. Nothing happened, not while I watched. There was no one there; I don't even think I was there. And it was cold. I came to a big monument with a statue of a man looking up at the sky and a plaque underneath. The plaque said, 'I hope only that with the short time available to us before this planet perishes, we shall be able to penetrate the surrounding darkness and make it possible for a precious few of our descendants to escape to another home for the human race, there to perpetuate a faint memory of those of us who rose from the slime and stood erect, in time to see the decay of our planetary system and our own imminent danger.'

It was just another of my coloured dreams. I can see it now, all I have to do is stop what I'm doing and I can see the cold luxuriance of colour and the brilliant severity of all that shining.

I hope you can get that part right. I don't want it to sound stupid. Better check your notes and see it makes sense.

The next day I listened in to a union meeting the workers held right underneath the stack in the shade. Boy, did they roast the boss. I bet anything you like they didn't talk like that in front of him, they probably said Mister and please and made their voices go nice and soft, trying to be educated. I don't know why but they always imagine a man in a collar and tie is educated, whatever that means. The head man was a fellow I knew from a big radio and electronics factory. He made a fortune out of FM equipment. I used to carry some of it for him round to a junkyard and he'd pick it up later that day and give me a few dollars for helping. He had to get the big end, he said, because it was his idea.

Back at the house they were all in bed. Actually, they were all in the same one, for the kids had all crowded in Bee's bed. I sat on the edge and I was surprised that Bee wasn't embarrassed, but then I remembered that she wouldn't know about that other girl the night before. She probably wouldn't have cared anyway, what was it to her? If she was determined to look after the kids, she'd do it no matter what I did.

One thing led to another and pretty soon all the rest of them were tickling each other and somehow I got mixed up in it and Bee ended up leaning against me while Stevo tickled her ribs with his cold little hands. He cocked his head to one side and said, 'What are you two doing wid lub?' He was only pretending, though, pretending we had leaned together on purpose. Actually I was a bit wary of putting my arm round her. I couldn't see her face, but suddenly I felt hot; there was a great cloud of gold hair all in my face. I sat still for too long, she must have wondered what was the matter, for she turned to look at me. We were pretty close, but it was still just fun. The kids were still there.

'Uh huh,' said Stevo. 'Lub and marriage.'

Bee was looking straight at my face, I didn't feel too comfortable; she usually got by without looking at me at all. I felt a bit like the time I visited Ma. I didn't have time to go and see her while she was in the other hospitals, not until she was in this little old private hospital at Balmoral; all she could talk about was the other women picking on her. They feel very persecuted when they're on the way out, they know life has turned against them. I tried to tell her not to take any notice, but it was no use, it was me she wouldn't take any notice of. And all the time she was looking straight at me.

Now that I've said it, it wasn't like that at all. I wanted to get away when Ma stared at me, but when it was Bee I wished I could shrink to nothing, almost, and walk safely along the beam of light from her eyes, right into her head. That would have suited me for a long, long time.

Bee wasn't a bit embarrassed, looking at me like that; she didn't say anything. Stevo rescued me, and boy, was I glad. I think I was a bit out of my depth then.

'I got a pain, Mum.'

61

'What sort of pain, darling?' You should have heard her voice when she said that word.

'A lovely soft kind of pain.'

She took off his pants and sent him to the toilet. I made her some instant coffee while she was dressing; I like coffee. I always feel very generous when I do anything for anybody; it doesn't happen often.

When Stevo came back Chris was giving Bee a cuddle, so Stevo put his arm round Chris to cuddle her, pushing Bee away with his free hand.

'Bubba and I are getting married; you've got Daddy.' I thought this was a pretty cunning move, separating Bee and Chris; maybe he'd be a politician. And later, when he saw Allie making for his dinkie, he directed her to Chris's toy pram.

He came and told us about it, though. 'I were bery sneaky,' he said. He knew we thought he was clever.

'Mummy,' said Chris. 'I going to kill Barry.' That was a kid next door. 'He hits me on the head, and kicks. I think I kill the whole family.'

'Perhaps we'd better not kill them,' advised Bee.

'You better not do them dead or they do you dead.' That was Stevo. Then he cornered me and started in on his story of the Chantic Bird.

'Once a king had a palace made of china so you had to be very careful if you touched it, and a garden so big it went right down to the sea. Even the gardener hadn't seen all of it.'

'What did a bird have to do with it?'

I knew he wouldn't tell me, he'd wait till he got to

62

it in the story. Into my head then came the sound of an owl's birdwing flap, and the funny sensation you get when you disturb fruit-bats and they fly in sharp angles, always missing you just when you think you're going to have a mess of leathery wing wrapped round your face.

You can't say I didn't listen to Stevo. But a little bit was enough, then I was off.

When I got back to the wheat stack, I only had a short sleep and when I woke up there was a man with lists, counting or pretending to count the different things in the yard. I knew it could easily be someone after me, trying to get close enough to grab me. If I had room to move, I'd run rings round them and they knew it, I'll bet.

I found something to do; I arranged the middle sacks so I could take them out, built them up high and leaned the outside sacks in towards the centre, so that the whole thing rested on one sack staying where it was, and there was only one corner of it supporting the ones above. When the man with the lists was counting some drums stacked near the fence, I pulled out the key sack and down she went. Nothing fell far, but the middle of the stack was a mess. It didn't make enough noise. When I looked back the man with lists was still there, counting.

6

POLICE STATION

I'm not much of a liar except when I believe it's the right thing to do, and I'd never been in jail before, anyway. This young copper found me asleep in a doorway and my pockets didn't jingle when he shook me, so he took me along. In the charge room they gave me a feel all over but found no folding money. Why should I own up? At least there was a roof on the place.

Old-time coppers would have given you a reef up the tail and told you to beat it, but promotion and their quota of convictions make them more savage nowadays. The old plastic pens were clicking away while they took down all the particulars I gave them.

Once you could have a bit of a stoush in the street and no one to worry, but now everyone's a private eye. First I thought they were picking me up because I did have a little fight earlier that night, and later a little target practice with the blue fluoro lights—you have to hit between the wires with little rocks to get a result—but it was just like them to lumber me when I was horizontal.

It was a pretty big station, and they had one of the crime cars there. Did you know there were only five in Sydney? For as far north as the Hawkesbury, south to Cronulla and west to Katoomba, five cars. That was good news. I was in a cell when they brought in two detectives that shot themselves in the leg. You get promotion when you're wounded—the police do—and these two came in with a story of how they both got shot in the leg chasing a crim in the fertile fields from Parra through to Blacktown. Both of them. Sometimes I could hardly hear what they said, I was listening through the wall, and the reason I couldn't hear was the old man in the cell with me. I could hear the noise he made with his lips on his teeth, a clucking noise, and when he moved the joints in his ankles, hips, back, shoulders, elbows, they all seemed to creak when he moved. And did he fidget! Boy, did he twist and shift; he bent down and straightened up, moved his head and his neck clicked; when he opened his mouth, for air, his tongue clicked from sticking to his teeth...I couldn't help hating crims, then. The caught ones. And when he sucked on a cigarette, the air sort of slipped past the paper and whistled into his mouth, like the bullets Ritcho used to fire at us little kids, whipping up the dust and splatting off the asphalt round our legs. But don't worry, I got Ritcho later. He liked garages and corner shops, so I hung round a garage a lot as if I was going to knock it off so he would see me, and sure enough, he tried to rob it. He had no idea of security, he got there on a pushbike! They took him away in a little blue van with wire over the back door.

The plainclothes brought in some weird stories. A barber shop burglary gave one of the detectives a bonus; the barber did something to one of the detectives and they had him up right away on a morals charge. Funny thing was, I knew that barber; he used to breathe right down your neck and make nice remarks about how you played football last Saturday. At least he sucked lollies for his breath. I really thought he was one. Poor cow must have been mad to lay a finger on a cop.

Then there was a shocker about a woman at Hargrave Park and her son. He was thirteen and tired as hell every day at school. His mate finally told his father and the father told the school and the school told the police; the mother used to put the boy on the kitchen table every morning. They'd brought her in the day before, and the detectives were telling the ones who hadn't heard and trying to make the newest young detective sick.

It made some of my little games seem like kids' stuff. I was proud of the one I did when I was younger, about fifteen. You rode along on your pushbike, downhill, until you saw a dopey sort of bloke in a car with enough other people in it to tell a different story for each person. You rode alongside the car, then you got close and fell down. It's easy when you do it a few times. The dopes stop and help. You either have someone waiting to jump them or you settle with them on the spot and threaten them there'll be cops if they don't. I didn't work with other kids, so I did the second one. I made fifteen quid off that, one Sunday. You never try that one on people that live near, only on strangers and sightseers.

They had me in over the weekend, so I had to wait till Monday to see the beak. It wasn't a bad place to sleep, once you were tired enough so the old men's noises didn't bother you. It was in jail I remembered being a kid in the bush and roasting eels and potatoes and snakes and millipedes over a fire. I didn't eat the millipedes, just watched them sizzle. They used to gather together in a cluster, all close together; I didn't like the way their bodies got so close together, all crawling over each other head to tail. Don't get me wrong, I don't mind that sort of thing now, but I was younger then. Just to show you how different I've got, I was in a 69 club for a few weeks; I don't join clubs or anything as a rule, but I joined this one just to see if the stories about it were true, and they were.

Anyway, the millipedes were all black and twisted together, you should have seen them untwist when the fire hit them. Even a match under them and they let go each other as if the next one was the cause of the heat. I got a lot of satisfaction watching that. It goes to show they didn't cling tighter together when their D-day came; they dropped each other quick smart, just like people.

I must have been young then. Do you know I went to a special opportunity class the last two years of primary school? It used to be called special classes, then opportunity classes, but just to make sure, people used both words and made it special opportunity classes. There I was, sixteen and three-quarter years of age, dozing off

67

in clink at Parramatta station, thinking about Artarmon school and millipedes. It doesn't make you think—I won't say that—but it's a funny thought to have and it could give you a bit of a laugh, if you felt like laughing. We had a teacher and one day when we were singing scales this teacher came round listening to us, jabbering that he could hear one voice clear as a bell. Clear as a bell, he kept saying it. You guessed it. Me. No bull, either. Old Mister Hocking certainly embarrassed me that day. I could have stopped, I suppose, but so what? Why shouldn't I feel what it's like to have someone get excited over me? After all, I was the only one that had the teacher help him buy books. My old man was doing pick and shovel then and there were plenty of us and we all ate like dogs. And I was the only one had to wear sandshoes in the winter, without socks. Socks wear out, and sandshoes were cheap. I had to give the books back, of course, but it was pretty decent of him. Them, I mean. We had another teacher, too. Pryce with a y and a long nose. He must have thought we were a lot of louses. We wouldn't have made jokes about the nose, or anything. Everyone has something stupid about them. I nearly said about him, but women are in this as well as those finished off with spouts.

These are the sort of things I used to turn over in my head at odd times, like the old blokes you used to see hanging around when you went to have a game of football. They'd always want to predict which of us could run, or play a good game, but they were never right. They picked the ones with thick legs as the runners, when they were second-rowers, and the tough looking ones as the tough ones, when they were just beat up. The kids with the flattest noses are the ones that dodge the fewest punches.

I can laugh about it now, and I did then in the cells, but my first smoking wasn't all that funny. You've picked up bumpers and spilled them out into cigarette papers or a twist of tissue paper. Everyone has. But doesn't it make your head spin? Specially when you take the bigger kids' advice and suck all the smoke down into your stomach.

The old fellow in the cell with me tried to stir the trouble-pot every time a constable brought us something to eat and every time one passed in the corridor. One of his favourite dodges was to talk about the desk-sergeant who got some tranquiliser made up and put in the morning coffee. The whole station was nice and quiet and the constables, even the detectives, walked about in a daze. When the supers and the brass called in, they liked the quiet, and you could see they thought the station was sort of holding its breath in awe. Coffee control, the old man called it. It was such a neat idea that I began to have a bit of respect for him. I won't say I liked him. When you hear of anyone liking anyone, you've got to suspect sex.

I got to thinking of how almost the whole world was against me and people like me. Or I was against the whole world. But where I beat them, they were so liberal minded they couldn't hurt me as much as I hurt them. The punishment was always easier on me than the crime was on them.

I can see me now, on their comfortable cop-shop bunk, looking at the black rust on the bars, thinking of when I was a kid; my first fight behind the water tank at Drummoyne, and waking up on the back verandah at my granma's place at Abbotsford looking up at my cousin's technical drawing of a thirty-eight engine and tender, looking out over the bay watching my aunt's ship coming in. Not that it came in, but she told me those masts I saw were it.

It's no wonder a fellow has no respect for people older than himself. They have too much, too much more than you have. They have time and money and words and a bagful of ideas to put over, more than a kid can cope with. And no one's on to them all the time, like they're on to us. We get too much publicity. People want to hear about us; we've driven the good boys out of the news.

The noise of the old fellow's sleeve against the brick wall woke me up. He was leaning over me, in another few seconds he would have ratted my clothes. He must have been able to smell the money I had hidden on me. Having someone bending over me like that reminded me of the old man bending over me and saying, 'I know you don't tell lies, do you?' I was too sleepy to hit the old bloke, just like I was too little to hit the old man, years ago. I just pushed him back a bit. He hit the other wall pretty hard.

Who got away with Ma's photos? I still don't know. And the others acted as if I took them, but I didn't. I wasn't lying, like I did to the old man. My face did it then, and having clear eyes. The old bloke told me they'd charge me with loitering. The old folks in charge of this world don't like you to be hanging about unless you're paid to do it, but the old crim was still trying to find out if I really had cash on me. His telling me that reminded me I might have to use a different style of speaking on Monday in front of the beak. They like you quiet, so they have to growl at you, or even have a good yell, to make you speak up. And you should be a bit slow, so they can follow what you're saying and pretend to be waiting for you.

They shifted the old fellow on Sunday and put two other kids in with me. They wanted me to go with them after I got out, and do a few jobs. But they had a leader and that ruled me out. Why do they always want leaders? They must like punishment, and being kept in line. I can't stand people in charge and I don't like to be in charge.

Let them do what they like, without me.

I wiped them, like a dirty nose.

When I got before the beak, I was first up on Monday, they wiped me just as quick when I fished out my roll of notes. If they knew where I got that money I'd have gone up for a million years, I bet. They even looked as if I could get a lawyer and take them to court. But I didn't mind, it was an experience. One thing, though. When I didn't take much notice of what the beak was saying, he said, 'Your brain is crippled.' What a thing to say! Anyway, I got out of there. My brain limped out after me.

Back at the house I found no Bee and no kids. I got up in the ceiling to have a secret sleep, but I was no sooner settled than one of Bee's neighbours came in. I thought it was Bee coming back and I made a noise getting down. It turned out to be one of Bee's friends. She came under the manhole I used, I could see her looking up. I didn't want her to see

71

my face, so when she called out I only grunted and got back up in the ceiling.

'Are you the electrician?' she called.

'The wiring,' I grunted, and didn't say any more.

'You won't be coming down for a while, will you?'

'No.' It was an old house and the manhole was right above the bath. This woman, she must have been some sort of nympho, started to peel off and have a bath. I know it was only because I was there.

'Hey,' I yelled down. 'Did Bee say you could do that?'

'She won't be back for an hour. She won't mind,' she said. 'You won't tell her I stole some hot water, will you?' She could tell I didn't want to meet her face to face; I suppose if she hadn't been sure of that, it would have been impossible to get near her with her pants off.

This woman went at last. She must have known where Bee was, because she only took half an hour over that bath, with me up there perving like mad. I heard the kids coming up the path ahead of Bee, who had to carry Allie. Chris must have seen some kid in a new dress, for she was complaining about her own.

'When can I have another dress?'

'That one's new enough,' said Bee.

'This is a filthy dress.' Filthy meant old. They were both like that, new meant clean and filthy meant old. Stevo was busy rousing on Robyn, a fat girl round the corner; so that's where they must have been.

Stevo said, 'You—you wrong number!' It was getting late; there'd only be a scratch tea. Bee locked no doors, anyone could have come in. Stevo made for the TV and turned it on. Bee clattered around in the sink, getting plates ready, opening drawers, throwing knives and forks around.

'Mummy! Stop doing that noise!' yelled Stevo. 'I'm reading the television.' Only he made it sound like terror-vision.

'Chris!' called Bee. 'Help me get Allie ready for bed.'

'She's not sleepy. Let her look at TV,' said Chris.

Stevo said, 'Bubby does want to go to sleep. She's got sleep all over her.' It may have been true, but he wanted to get rid of her and have the set to himself. That was clear enough to his sister, she made noises and the tears appeared right away.

'Don't get upcited, Chris,' Stevo said. 'Don't get upcited.' I got down quietly, remembering the noise I made before, and crept up behind the kids in the lounge room. I thought I was going to scare them, but they were used to me. They expected me to jump out of dark corners. The way they said hullo made me feel good, though.

When we'd had tea, Stevo cornered me again and told me the Chantic Bird from the beginning again and got a bit further than before. The littlies curled up like commas on the floor. First there was the King with his china palace and his garden big as a country. Then he said how travellers came from a long way off to look at the palace and gardens, but they all ended up liking the Chantic Bird, which was way down by the sea and used to sing to the fishermen. Great writers and poets, the wisest men in their countries, even came and saw and wrote about the Chantic Bird, and their books went round the world. The last to read about the bird was the King, and what he read was that the best thing in his country, better than the china palace and the garden of a thousand miles, was the Chantic Bird.

'Why didn't I know this?' asked the King. 'Get me this bird.'

I laughed at that, because the very first day I brought home from school my card from the Gould league of bird-lovers, I took out the old BB gun and got my first bird, a sparrow on the clothes-line. But no one in the palace knew about the bird, even though it was famous in every other country in the world. And no amount of punishment or promises could make anyone produce it. They would soon have to look for their information among the poorer classes because when they did they would come across the pretty little kitchen-maid who knew all about the bird.

I could see Stevo was pleased to be telling me so much of his story, so I decided to let him leave some pleasure for next time. Lucky I brought two bags of chips with me; I gave him one and one to Bee for Chris, then off. Actually I went first and changed the metho for my great-grandfather's eye.

Did I tell you about the eye? He got it torn out in a fight—yes, that's the one—and shoved it back in and went after the other bloke. Well, the eye is still in the family. The old man didn't like the idea of keeping it, but he kept it anyway when we begged him to. People, even fathers, always like you to beg. You had to keep changing the metho every few months, otherwise it got all brown and cloudy. I'm glad it didn't end up in some hospital incinerator with the amputations and tonsils and things.

I didn't keep it where Bee might get it.

*

Next day a brown bomber—a parking cop—gave me a fright. I came round a corner slap bang into him, then later on one was following me. Being in jail hadn't done me any good. I was getting nervous. The first time I ducked into a doorway, the second time I stepped off the footpath between two cars without thinking, and only the sound of a hellicking great rusty bulldozer saved me from going under it.

I hate uniforms very much, and walked along by myself as usual, hating them all day. And thinking. Actually the only way I could stop suffocating was to keep away from people. With too many around too much of the time it was as if there couldn't be enough air for me to breathe.

Did those two people, who might have been strangers to me if I hadn't been their son, did they enjoy it when they had me, or rather when they started me? Or did they slog away for hours, hating it? Trying again each month when they missed, getting nastier...

7
TENT

A tiny bit of light came through the bush at me and a huge
bellow started a sort of echo, a tingling echo, in my chest.
The light was the tiny shout of a match flaming, the shout
was the huge flaming of a very red man in a check shirt and
open chest. There'd been a racket coming from this other
camp, they must have been drinking dozens of bottles of
grog and now they were singing. The red man had an open
chest, since not only was his check shirt open, but a round
red opening had appeared on the skin of his chest. What it
was, they shot him in mid-song. Dead silence contradicted
his cheerful racket.

Maybe someone only let off the rifle to get rid of a
shell. Since it was night and the man had been shot by
matchlight and there was little or no campfirelight, I got
closer, and while they were still shocked at what they'd

done and scrabbling at their things to get away, I pinched their tent. The whole tent. Pegs and all. Pulled it out of the ground and off. The man with the rifle was busy stuffing dirt and gravel down it, ready to loose another shot and put different markings on the inside of the barrel. I suppose he'd burn off the stock on the fire.

I felt suddenly pink and gold. And found myself running again. I knew that track and folded the tent in my arms while I was running. I decided to turn the feeling off, but I couldn't; I hoped it wouldn't make me spend my energy before I was safely camped, but there was nothing I could do. I felt so good, I knew I would have to wait until I calmed down.

Miles away I got the tent up. I was feeling pretty gold, but I'd lost my pink a bit, so I lay right down to go to sleep. I knew like that I'd never feel cold no matter what blew up from the south.

On a night like that you could hear the tree bark growing, and light airs would come over the dry hills and hum very quiet in the tree leaves, and far down in the valley you could hear the little creek that came and went from nothing to waterfalls, making its talk over the rocks and cold stones. Even though I felt good I couldn't help thinking that even the winking little stars have rough edges, that look so smooth a few light years away.

My funny warm feelings must have coloured in my dreams that night. I even dreamed I was in the bush. While I can still dream, I am me. Down where three valleys met and the cool sound of water and the quiet bark of the trees made it my private theatre, a singer stood on a rock surrounded by the green and amber of young, moist leaves. He sang a slow song, very sweet, it made a funny feeling on top of my head and suddenly I felt cold, and shivered. I still seem to hear what he sang. In my dream I knew that was the sort of song that made a bit of wet come into my eyes, the next thing I had some tears gathering up to make their own private waterfall down from my eyelids.

When I woke up cold just before dawn for my usual reason, I thought that no matter what was outside my tent, all I had to do was go inside and I could imagine myself alone on a desert with nothing but rocks and bones and prickly ants for company. Or like one of those explorers that get time off from their bosses, I could imagine myself on top of a mountain with the wind slashing through and round and under, with nothing but snow and age-old granite for company.

When that thought hit me, I picked up a lump of rock and I looked at it hard, trying to pretend I could see it, looking close at the grains stuck together that made them all together a rock, and thinking how blasted old it must be. And the rest of it, that this bit broke off from, and so on. How simply old; stinking, stupid, unreasonable old...Thinking like that made me throw the rock as far as I could, and when it landed the last shadow of my dreams and thoughts vanished.

On the way back to the house to have a game with the kids, I made a few of my special traps in the paddocks I crossed. You dig round holes and cover them with cowcakes. People tread in them and twist their ankles or just fall over. It's great fun doing it and laughing about what might happen. I carried a few cakes in my shirt and when I'd dug some holes in footpaths I lidded them with cowcakes. Nice, dry, thin ones. I couldn't wait to see them in action, though I thought I'd like to spend a few hours at the house with Bee and the kids.

First I thought I'd get them a lot of vegetables cheap, because there was a glut at the markets, but no go. I suppose they were dumping their potatoes at sea as usual, and the farmers that couldn't get their things to market were ploughing them in. You hope that some things might have changed, but they don't change.

When I got there next door's cat was on the verandah sunning his claws, and Stevo was in the middle of telling Bee how a dog had followed him to school. He wasn't too happy with strange dogs.

'Were you scared?' asked Bee.

'I shaked a bit,' said old Stevo. 'He stopped and did wee-wee a lot.'

I played cricket with him in the backyard. Chris and Allie got in the way a bit and pretty soon there was yelling and shrieking. It never bothered me, but Bee got sharp. She abused Chris and Allie and Stevo as well as me. I knew she didn't mean it, she was just yelling because we were out there and she wasn't.

'Come and get on the end of this bat!' I yelled, and out she came. She was all right, too. Her brothers were all cricketers.

'When I grow up, I just want a good wife who won't yell at the kids,' said Stevo. That flummoxed Bee. She went over and put his head against her stomach—actually it went a little way into her stomach; she had a very soft one—and patted him. That flummoxed Stevo. Funny thing, when you looked close at it, his skin had much the same patterns mine had. Mine had more brown, that's all. The game stopped. Bee went inside and made some jelly for the kids. I showed the kids how to tie Allie up without hurting her.

'You can't tie up Bubba. Her my best friend.' Stevo was firm. Another game gone west. Bee started stirring the jelly, you could hear it easily. Stevo raced in to help.

'Ha, red jelly and green jelly. I like jelly.'

'That's not green, that's yellow,' said Bee,

'Yellow, is it? All right, that'll do,' said Stevo. The colour of the red jelly was just the colour of the thumb I saw a butcher cut off one afternoon at Parramatta while I watched in his window.

So while I had nothing to do I told him about living. You know what I mean, you had to explain to kids, the way my parents didn't, that there's a time before each of us lived, a time while we live and a time after we live. A lot of miserable people think a lot too much about the hellishing big time after we live, but it's just as long a time before we lived, so what's the difference?

'Where was I before I was in Mummy's tummy!' Stevo buttonholed me.

'Wouldn't have a clue, Stevo,' I admitted. 'But the point is, once upon a time there was no Stevo, now there is a Stevo, and one time later there won't be any Stevo.'

'Will you be gone too?' he observed.

'I'll be gone long before you, matey,' I emphasised. 'Like the trees. Dogs up the street. The mossies. This house. There's a time before everything was, then a time for it to live, then it ups and dies.'

'Does everything have a turn?'

'Everything that gets here has a turn. A turn to be born, and when it's time to die, it dies. A house falls to bits.'

'And dogs leave their chin-bones down the bush,' he added. We'd come across part of a dog skull on a rubbish heap near the scouts' camp.

'Sure,' I agreed. 'Trees fall down. Mossies get slapped. Houses get bulldozed or you put a match to them.'

Bee didn't mind me talking to him. I could tell she wanted me to take more notice of the kids. I suppose there will come a time when they roll her down with the Rookwood clay, or some other clay, and what was once a person will become a nothing. But Stevo was thinking, too.

'Daddy, a lot of things trouble me.'

'Don't think about it,' I advised. 'Come and have a shot with your gun.'

He got out his BB gun and we took it outside and blasted away fiercely at a book my old man left behind. It was a book of Kipling stories with nice thick paper that didn't make the BB's go oval. You could use them again. I taught him little things like that in case I wasn't always there to pinch bullets for him. And guns. I think it's better if they don't know where the goodies come from, but you've got to make sure they're not altogether helpless in case some bottle or bullet or drunken bum takes you off stage before you expect to go.

Stevo was really getting the idea of guns. You should have seen him, with one eye shut tight and the other straining to line up the sights. He was too young to get him to relax. It made me feel a better bloke to see him getting fierce and strong and joyful, and aiming straight.

And the things he said! When the phone rang—when I was ringing up Bee—and there was a letter came for me, which wasn't often, he yelled over the phone, 'Here's a letter for you, look!' And when the day was narrowing down to a last few things to be put away, with bed next, he would say, 'Put things away! Put things away! Why I have to do all these jobs?' I liked him saying those things you wouldn't expect to hear any old time, especially times when he was cranky at having to do something. He was like me. As soon as anyone wanted to tell me what to do or how to do it, that was the finish. I knew what had to be done and I knew what I wanted to do. Other people might not like it, but they weren't me.

Stevo was a good kid when he knew what he did pleased Bee.

'Now we'll get Bubby to bed,' Bee would say.

'All right. If that's the way you want it.' That was Stevo. I suppose I don't really want him to get like me. Some of the things I believe in wouldn't help him. Like idleness. You know, not doing the sort of things the authorities like. Idleness, the way I do it, is a counterpunch to all their rush; they're going nowhere anyhow, the real important work in this world is done inside people, with no one watching. Besides, I can never stop hearing a sort of inside laughter that tells me beyond the next heart beat there may be nothing.

When we'd fixed him up with some hot water to splash about in, Bee told me something he said that day. She'd been trying to get them dressed first thing that morning and she didn't feel too bright, but she tried not to yell and screech at them.

Stevo remarked to her, 'Sometimes when you talk it's like crying.' She thought that was pretty funny. I did too.

After their bath, Bee made me listen to the Chantic Bird. Made me. Stevo went over it all from the start, about the china palace and the garden of a thousand miles and the foreigners who came and praised everything, but praised the Chantic Bird, most of all. And how no one in the tinkling palace knew where to find the bird with the chantic song.

How did she make me listen? Stevo was getting into his stride and there was a very bright sort of light over his face because when he smiled he smiled with his whole face, and he didn't see what Bee was up to. But she'd walk in and out, listen a bit, stop, turn around, and come back. It kept me off balance. Usually she knew where she was going, exactly. She went straight to something and what she did was definite. I suppose I'm a bit like a wild animal, sort of on the look out for aimless movements, signs of bewilderment, the sort of vagueness and weakness that I could move in on, and I'd say she knew it. But what got me even more than seeing her not know what she was about, was the sight of her pretty pink heels. She had on these skimpy little slippers—she didn't have great sheila's feet; she was small and neat, with no twists and burred over toes—and the slippers showed her clean feet, all pink, a very delicate pink, and it got me. Mostly she dressed right up to the neck,

83

it seemed to me, compared to the sluts I was used to, but now she'd scraped off her lip colouring and pulled her hair back from her ears and the white part of her neck under her hair. I could have eaten any part of her. And when she passed near me she suddenly let loose her hair and I was suffocated in honey gold.

That's how she made me sit and listen. When I say sit and listen I actually mean just listen, because I don't sit for very long, I have to move around, even if it's only from one foot to another. I guess I think I'll be fixed in one spot if I stop for too long.

Stevo was up to the part where they asked the kitchen maid and she said, 'Yes. I know the Chantic Bird very well. She lives by the sea and when she sings, the tears come in my eyes.'

'Silly girl,' they said. 'Take us to the bird, the King must hear it.' On the way, the officials heard cows mooing and thought that was the bird; they heard frogs and said, 'That's the bird.' But they only thought they knew what they were listening to. Then the Chantic Bird sang, and the girl pointed to her proudly. But all they saw was a little grey bird. The Chantic Bird sang beautifully, but they were not impressed; they were disappointed she didn't have pretty feathers.

'Will you sing for the King?' said the kitchen maid.

'Yes,' said the Bird, 'but I'd sooner stay in the green trees by the sea.'

Pretty soon, when Bee thought Stevo had had a fair crack of the whip, she made herself scarce. She knew I'd go if there was nothing solid to stay for. I told Stevo that was enough for that night and I'd see him tomorrow. He got a sort of questioning look in his eye like when his leg got burned, just before the pain hit him.

I'm always doing that. I suppose my brother that died must have looked at me like that when I'd visit him once in a blue moon, then go after five minutes. I was there when he died, though. If I could have got to him later when his face was setting, I would have changed his expression into something fierce and knowing, and got rid of his bewildered and helpless look.

Thinking about these things shoots me. Personal integrity, the value of work, consideration for others, good manners, all the things Stevo was learning, all the things my brother's death and my parents' death made me think of, I know they're good and all that. But sometimes I can't stand them. Thinking of them makes me want to spew. The ideas I get to trick people and do what I like, I bet the ordinary bloke only gets those ideas when his woman Noes him or when sickness, accident or death back him up against a wall.

I got back near my tent. I hung around a while before going right up to it, because of natural animal caution. Just as well, too. A man and a woman were standing a hundred yards away and I could see they were edging near it, looking for a place to lie down. I let them go, so what? I didn't even feel like sneaking up on them. They looked around a lot and at last ducked their heads and went in. The sides flapped, I guess they were taking their clothes off. That made me curious, so I crept up on them, but I wasn't really feeling like it.

85

Sure enough, they had their clothes off and what they were doing would make you laugh. There I was, sixteen and three-quarters, and I knew how to do properly what they were trying to get round to. The woman at the riding school that got me into the 69 club was an Einstein compared to these bunglers.

Suddenly I was disgusted. I wouldn't admit it to myself, but the sight of Bee's pinkness still had me. If I couldn't have her, why should these old lovers have any peace? I eased the pegs out of the ground till they were all holding by an inch, then when I was ready I lifted the main stay right out of the ground and let go. Canvas collapsed over them. I walked away, I knew they couldn't chase me naked. Besides, I didn't feel like running, for once.

I was still in the bush when this feeling closed round me, just like the tent closed round the man and woman. I had sense enough to get off the main track on to a tiny clearing where I could get off my feet. Suddenly I've got no energy and all I want to do is sleep.

86

8
BOAT

All of a sudden, on my way out to the jetty, I got these big thumps in the chest. I had to stop and bend over, breathing in like mad, but I didn't seem to get any air. Something was certainly twisted in there. I didn't feel funny in the head, so I must have been getting blood up there all right, just a mix-up in the chest. I leaned, I sat down, I sat back, I lay flat. While the swirling got dizzier in my chest, I straightened up, lifting my head and saw a cloud in the sky and the little patch of cloud I was looking at seemed to rush down into my eyes so that wherever I turned my head all I could see was the thick of a cloud. I don't know how long it lasted, but you've got to take your mind off yourself, so I looked round the sky and the clouds, trying to imagine the whole of the universe. The water sounds, lapping at the crusty old piles of the jetty, were silly compared to the silence you could see right up there as far as eye-power could take you. I realised I was nothing, dumped on a putrid mound of nothing, ready to get under the mound as soon as I am putrid, too.

Is it a sort of happiness that moves the sun and the stars? There must be a lot of things that words can't stretch enough to fit round. There must be a lot of words waiting to be born to attach themselves to things we feel are near us. I rubbed my chest a bit, but I soon stopped rubbing and thinking. A piece of my fingernail had got split at the edge and it kept catching in my nylon shirt. It got me on edge so much I had to get up and tell myself I felt a lot better. What I did, I took this boat out and rowed it round the point till I got to another bay and when I saw a fishing boat that had just got in, tied up at a wharf and the men gone ashore for a drink before they unloaded, I found a thing to do. I put the fish that moved over the side and let them swim away. I left enough for the men's dinner, allowing enough for two men.

That didn't make me feel much better, though, because that hangnail kept getting in my shirt, or catching in the ropes or in the canvas. It nearly drove me mad.

The boat I pinched wouldn't be used or missed until the weekend, so in the meantime it was an ark for me, somewhere to rest and sleep in the sun. Late afternoons, though, heading it into the sun, I was a Viking in a Viking ship and I stood up front. I know you call the front the bow and a boat is a she, but that's when you're tied to the sea. I couldn't have cared less about the sea or the boat, even though I liked it for a few days, so I didn't reckon it was right to pretend to a love for it that I didn't have. I know

88

that's a funny sort of way to be honest, but I'd rather be honest to myself than to anyone else.

I got the hangnail down, rubbing it flat on the wood at the edge of the boat, where the paint had come off.

I put in where there was about fifty yards of beach, and walked up to a pub to have a few beers. There were some kids around my age and big like me, so I got talking to them. But the noise kept getting louder and louder, heads were beginning to spin and barmaids starting to short-change the drunks, and one of the kids started falling off his bar stool and when they went out for some fresh air and gave a driving lesson to one that couldn't drive, I could see I ought to clear out, since I liked the boat I'd pinched and didn't have any use for their utility truck. What they did, they started up and the one at the wheel was so drunk he headed straight for the little cliff they had there just above the water. To get that far, he had to go between two big gums and miss another one, so I jumped off the back. When they stopped and went through a little white fence that was a memorial to some locals who got killed in the war and knocked the statue in half at the legs so there were just these two legs standing up, and one of them who'd been asleep in the back got out and saw what had happened and threw up his fish and chips on the grass out of giddiness, I off.

It's no use trying to team up with other blokes. It never works, not even with a few beers aboard. I cast off and headed back to this jetty I know, and since it was a nice night, I had a lay down on the planks. I thought it wasn't as much fun knocking statues about if you couldn't do it all yourself.

It's not that I'm afraid of other kids. I'm not afraid of *anything* I can yell at. What gets me is inside. I'm being sniped at from inside and all the bullets are hits. Whoever is inside me, sniping, has no misses.

The sound hit my ear first. I put my head right down to the old adzed plank and what I heard got me over the side into the boat and cast off in about two shakes of a bird's tail. The prawners were out. There were so many tins rattling and things, they didn't hear me, but pretty soon they would see me.

They didn't, though. I kept away from them on the dark side of the river, there were only two of them, and later when I drifted the boat round back to the jetty, I got a few handfuls of prawns and one of their empty tins and anchored the boat later across from Lane Cove and went to sleep with tomorrow's lunch beside me.

I cooked them ashore next morning in the tin with some sea water, I had no other salt, cooked them till they just turned pink. Delicious. The blackberries were out, so I ate till I rumbled. They left my mouth mainly sweet, but there was a sharp sourness down my throat. It must have been someone's land, because this man came up through the bush, you could hear him half a mile away, but I didn't go like he said. How can a man own dirt and rocks and she-oaks and mangroves? If you had to move every time someone said you were standing on their property, you'd have to suspend yourself a foot above the ground, even then you'd be violating their airspace. You can't all live together on the skin of the world if you have to keep off every place owned by someone. Who hands out the right to own bits of the planet?

He wasn't big enough to get too close to me, but I didn't want to scare him enough for him to get help—I wasn't finished eating—so I started chatting about early history. I'm not completely ignorant. There was a place called the Butcher's Block near there in Tambourine Bay; someone gave it to someone in the early days with an axe or a chopper or something. You'll find it in any history around the times of Mary Reibey. This man didn't seem to know too much about it. He wasn't interested in history, only title-deeds.

Finally he sat down and sulked, waiting for me to go. I told him I wouldn't hurt him, but when I went over to talk to him man to man, he scooted back into the brush. As if he had protection there. So then I pretended I was a bit of a woolly-woof. I invited him out in the boat with me, I even started lowering the old strides. Ready to flash it. That got rid of him. You'll know better than I do how eager everyone is to deny he shares any of the naughty ideas that homosexuals get lumbered for, but did you ever spend a couple of minutes watching these same blokes, miserable at home with Mumma, but faces shining like new pennies with their mates, punching each other lightly when they look as if they'd rather be holding hands, yelling belligerently at their mate when what they'd like to do is coo and kiss.

It's everywhere, I tell you. I see it all around me. But as far as thinking about what you might do, anything is possible. Anything at all. You can't trust yourself not to do a certain thing. You don't know what you'll do.

*

91

I got away from there and round to Fuller's Bridge and went for a bit of a run through the bush and that made me feel better. What cheered me up, too, was having to hurdle a blanket. This little dip in the track, a tiny valley, and at the bottom of it a man and a woman in a blanket. When I say in, they were really wrapped. I reckon they were taking a day off work, there was a little tinny English car on the main track two hundred yards away, I thought of taking it, but I was so pleased to see two natural people together that I let them have their car. They'd be tired, later, what with all their hugging and things.

I enjoy jogging through the bush. Did I tell you? One of my favourite things is to walk or jog on a bush track or even across country and let my head go on thinking. Now and then you stop and if it's summer you chew a sarsaparilla leaf or grab a handful of wild currants—they're very sour and they bring all the juices up from the lower side of your tongue and make it tickle. Or the nutty parts of those woody things that look like fat mountain devils; you have to split them on a rock and you eat the black kernel with the white inside.

I remembered Stevo saying, 'Would you buy me a Captain John hat and clothes so I can be happy?' A lot of the things I think of come from the house and Bee and the kids. We used to live at Lane Cove once, I remember trying to make boomerangs out of the mangroves across the river from Ludowici's.

Back to the boat in a big circle, no one had touched it, and when I picked up the frayed rope I tied up with, I thought of Stevo asking could he help me paint the roof.

You tied a rope to a verandah post, threw it over the iron roof and pulled yourself up the other side. He wanted to help on the roof.

'I will do it, for I can do a really good, hard, splendid job,' he testified. I had to tell him the iron was too hot, and just to make him feel he was still a man, I gave him the girl guide's knife I found at school once and the pair of black hockey pads. Actually, I found them a little before they were lost.

And when I came down for lunch that day—I don't know how Bee got me painting that roof—she had ready a pastry thing with fluffy white lolly on top called meringue. Stevo asked, 'Can I have some of that? And if I like it, I'll beg you for some.'

Bee used to say he was a dear little kid and that always used to make me feel peculiar, but I used to make myself remember he was my brother and only little, and the peculiar feeling went away.

We got the works that day. Stevo not only got some of that lolly stuff, he got jelly. Boy, could he put jelly away.

'Jelly gives me strength,' he used to reckon. 'Come on, let's fight before I lose my jelly!' And he'd punch and swing like mad, head down, a roundhouse swinger.

When I was a kid a retired minister took us away for a holiday to Wamberal. We'd never had a holiday before, and there was a kid there about my age now, and I used to get him to fight with me, just like Stevo did with me. I wish I'd had an older brother to fight with and play ping-pong with.

There was a little kid that was going to get what he wanted, that Stevo. Listen to what he said once to get himself another drink of milk. He went up to Bee, not too close, and started to lecture her.

'Are you thinking of God, or silly things?' He'd just been to Sunday school. 'God is the law around here, around the world. Even the Indians and medicine men and natives pray to God. And God said I can have some milk!' That slayed her. He got the milk. If she hadn't given it to him, I would have.

I carved a small stone face of a boxer I knew for Stevo, then next we found that he and the kids had made it Jesus. That's when we sent them to Sunday school; after that they stopped the Jesus bit and called it General Thunderbolt, their leader; reporting, saluting. Even the kids had to have leaders.

Some houses were opposite then and putting my hands up to my eyes with a little hole through each one I pretended to myself I had binoculars up, searching the bedroom and bathroom windows for naked girls and wives like I used to do when I was a kid peering in at Phyllis Jensen in her bath, singing like mad. She was, not me. I had a lay down in the boat, listening to the water flapping the side, pretending to myself it was the small, dry rustle of the half-dead grass under the girls' dressing sheds where I used to look up through the cracks. I won't tell you where, or you might go there and get caught. Boy, was I full of lewd imaginings that day.

I got those funny words when I read a paper one day about a court case. I don't often read papers, I think they take the edge off anyone wanting to do anything. And they never show anyone living a happy life. They never give someone's name, someone like me, and say how colossal he enjoys life and what a good time he has doing just what he wants. No sir, not one stinking word of all the happy clowns like me.

My boat nearly hit a launch about then. There was no bump, I saw it in time and did what had to be done, but the people in the launch bawled out as if you'd taken their lollies. They had a radio going full blast, which was bad taste, I thought. As if the nice noise of the water wasn't enough. That took me back to when Bee said she sometimes couldn't sleep for the noise. The old man next door was deaf and couldn't afford a hearing thing in his ear, but they were lucky I pointed it out to them before it annoyed me, too. They might have been sore and sorry and a lot worse off.

Bee's funny. She's got her own way of thanking you. After I did that, she didn't say anything, although blind Freddy could see I did it for her, and she stopped telling me if things got on her works. Sometimes I tried to think up things that might be worrying her, but I don't have much luck at things like that. It is hard to do other people's worrying for them. When Bee didn't look too severe, Stevo would test her and grab something she would use next and start to take it away.

'Don't do that,' she'd say. 'I want it.'

'You cry about it. Go on,' he'd command.

I put in to a nice sandy cove, mostly because I wanted to relieve myself. The noise of the boat beaching, however, sent a party of lovers in all directions. That was a fine time to come across four pairs of kids taking a day off work, but just to put them at their ease I went then and there on the sand instead of searching round in the trees and rocks. I could feel them watching me from the bushes and behind rocks. They still didn't show themselves; they must have been very shy kids, so all I could do was go. There was no sense in destroying their day, they probably worked in Sydney and needed a day off now and then apart from their weekends, which were likely strenuous enough.

There was not even a titter from them and no attempt to attack me, so I didn't muck up their clothes or take their transistors, but they could at least have given me a look at them. All I saw moving behind a thin red gum was a bottom, and it turned out to be a boy's. The age of that bottom was around sixteen, so they were all probably past the beginner stage. I didn't bother to think about what their parents would say if they knew where they were instead of being off at the pictures in town, like they probably said, but now that I remember it there is a funny side to it.

I put out again, a bit disgusted. If they were that shy, why make a party of it? I stopped thinking of them a few yards off shore and when I looked back without actually thinking of it, there they were at it again. Don't expect me to tell you where, but if you like to take a boat up the Parramatta, exploring the whole line of shore, you'll be very surprised at the nooks you find.

My head went back to the house where Bee was making a fuss at Stevo. You can bet he deserved it, though; she didn't pick on them for next to nothing, like most women.

'Do you love me, Mummy?' he enquired, when she stopped for breath. 'Or are you still upcited?' By that time I was thinking I was missing them, so I ditched the boat near a road not far from Halvorsen's sheds and got a train back home. You don't need a ticket on these trains, all you do is jump off the back carriage, cross the lines out of sight, and up the embankment. They don't bother to chase you when they see you're young and can probably run. When I bowled in, there was Stevo just as I'd last seen him in my head.

'Want a look at my composition, Dad?' he questioned.

'Sure, kid.' I'd forgotten what compositions looked like almost. He dragged out a ten by twelve sheet of paper and shoved it at me. The letters were about an inch high, he wasn't a very good writer. But then again, I wasn't, and it never worried me.

> This is my pet.
> My pet is a orange bird.
> It can fly, and fly high.
> I feed my pet and I like
> To play with him.

There was a picture of the orange bird at the bottom. Orange was his favourite colour. Mine is yellow.

'More story, Dad?' he requested, and I said yes without bothering to think, so he gave it to me from the start. I was looking for a sight of Bee and something to keep me there, but she must have decided I'd have to be interested just for the story's sake, because she didn't appear.

Stevo started out with the tinkling china palace, the miles of garden, the wise men and their books about the Chantic Bird and how the King wanted the Bird and the kitchen maid took them to the little grey bird by the sea. When they brought her back to the King, everyone sat round to listen to the song. She sang so sweetly that the King cried real tears, and everyone was touched by the song but watched the King to see what he would do. 'It is like glass bells ringing,' said the King, and the Bird sang more.

When he got up to reward the Bird, they did too. But the King really appreciated the beauty of the song; however, he knew nothing of the beauty of freedom, especially the freedom of a bird to sing in its natural home of green trees by the water. He gave the Bird a special cage and allowed it out twice a day, but a dozen hangers-on were there to see she did not fly away home. There was even a rope—a silken rope, but still a rope—tied to each leg when she flew out twice a day for exercise.

I'd heard enough story, so I gave Stevo a bag of lollies I'd bought, and off. Why couldn't Bee have come around with just a bit of skin showing—a hand, her neck, anything? Just to keep me interested. I couldn't help thinking of all the bodies on the ground at Berowra and Hornsby and Parramatta park, all over the place, anywhere there was a patch of dark ground, so thick on the ground you couldn't step between them, and here was me had to knock a sheila down before I did any good, and had to wait around like a spider to catch a sight of Bee, the girl I'd known since I was a kid. The upshot was, I got miserable.

When did I start? Did they do it hating each other? Did that kid that used to pee off the back verandah or through a hole in the verandah floor, did that kid have to grow up to be me? The one that photographed his mates peeing into a peaches tin at National Park and told the chemist he'd better develop the film or else he'd have no windows.

Allie and Chris havocked the saucepans just then, and the cake dishes, flour sifters, biscuit pans and baking dishes, and the kitchen was a mass of aluminium from end to end. By the time Bee got there, I was away.

The boat was still there, so I didn't have to go looking for another one. I had just got it off the Parramatta River mud and a bit of keelroom under me, when this big covered motor boat hailed me and wanted me to help him moor it. He was alone on the boat and I'm just about to give him a hand when I said to myself, I went easy on those kids before, why should I be always helping people? So I stood up in the boat and thought a bit and while I was thinking I picked up some flat stones from the bottom of the boat and skimmed them over the water. The best I did was seven hits, that is, when I skimmed it, it hit the water and bounced up again seven times. I decided this man in the boat might be the fellow I thought was following me; I noticed someone before, if you remember, sort of driving me out of whatever place I was in, stopping me from settling down in any place. Sure as I thought I was right, there he'd be right on me.

No one can be a nice free island with no one bothering you; everyone has to be nothing more than a bit of dirt along with everyone else. I turned away from that stupid man—let him tie up his own boat and get his feet wet—and since it was getting on to the afternoon, I decided to do something spectacular, as soon as I could get an audience.

What I did, I heaped the boat with brush and gum leaves and went back downstream until I came to a place where there were factories and I could get near the shore. I waited till it was about five to four and the workers were in the yards waiting for the knock-off whistle. Then I headed her upstream into the afternoon sun and had a Viking's funeral.

What you do is heap the brush so you can be standing behind a half-circle of it and when you light it and the brush burns and the gumleaves smoke like blazes, you appear to be standing right in the middle of it. From the other shore, of course, they can see you're behind it, but the ones near me didn't know.

Just before I set fire to it I heard the last lathe or power saw or milling machine, or whatever it was, turned off, and there was a new quiet on the water. My bonfire crackled and smoked and the sun lit me up like Technicolor. People in the waterside streets stopped and pointed and some ran inside to telephone to get the dollar from the papers, the dollar you never get. They always say someone else rang first. All I did was stand still—that always rattles people, they think you're looney if you stand still—and head west into the sun.

It wasn't as much fun as it could have been if a lot of people had been after me. I just went past them, pretty glorious of course, but out of reach.

The workers looked at me through their wire fences. They couldn't chase me, though. They weren't allowed out.

9

BRIDGE

Don't ever pal up too close with girls. You get too dependent on them. It's like a tall kid and a short kid, with the tall kid bending down all the time so as to be the same height as the short kid and not to make him miserable, then the tall kid finding it hard to straighten up to his natural height again when he needs to. Girls shorten you down to their size.

They're cunning, too. Ever notice how healthy a girl is before you get thick with her, then when you're saddled with her, she feels free to get sick all the time, and slops back to what she must have been before she put on the act? I get tired of girls very smartly.

I hope I can keep this story sort of kind, with no hard feelings for anyone in it. Or am I kidding myself? Is it ever going to be possible for me to be kind to others, when I have to suffer these hittings in the chest that come from nowhere and rock my whole body? When they come I can sit down and look at my chest and stomach and see them shake with each heart beat, and my head shakes too, so that my eyes seem to flicker if I'm trying to look steady at any one thing.

Other times everything is different and I'm on top of the world; the only thing left to beat is myself. But whether it's good times or rotten times I'm caught up in this sort of hurricane that doesn't rest, hurrying me on, knocking me here and there. Pursued by people I can't quite sight properly, that dodge out of the way just as I'm trying to focus on them, and the thought bashing me in the head, on and off, that there is something waiting for me in the future, something not good.

I forget where I was then, but I remember the sound of a peewit's wings, fast-flapping wings, scaring off crows. Then later, I remember closing my eyes, just as if I was on the back of a train, and seeing the receding column of the present as it may have been, except I didn't see it. I was looking at the receding past. That was a depressing thought; I started to think there was no such thing as the present time, only the nearest piece of the past instead. Where was I?

I remember, too, the sound of a turning car, and the croak of a rubber suspension bush. Then I was on a train. I remember that. There was the green painted leather of the seats, and there was me sitting back thinking about I was only ever caught once doing bad things and making a resolution to go back and get that rotten interferer, but it came back to me that I already did. He was the one

I waited for when he was on the way home from the pub at Penno.

In the train, that's where. Two men arguing behind me about the coalition of the Liberal and Country political parties, and were they getting stuck into each other. I was turning around to shut them up and I found it was one man. Talking and arguing to himself and taking two parts. I looked at him hard to see if he was kidding me, but no, he didn't even stop. He had no blank look in his eyes like some people find in loonies' eyes; they were bright and he looked very interested in what he told himself. A couple of kids with big cases got on, I remember that; they looked as if they were running away from home. One had a violin. They sang madly a lot of the way. I still can't remember where I was, perhaps I'd had some sort of blackout, I'd know if I'd been on the grog; it's no use, it won't come back to me. Yes, the train passed a station where a man and a woman were doing something under the railway steps. It was afternoon and her coat was wrapped round him; that much has come back.

Oh, and the noise of shunting.

I'll tell you what is handy, and that's a bit of leather from train seats. It's good stuff and even though they mark it now, there's a lot of things it's handy for. I slashed a few and got some good squares, just the sort of thing to pin down on the old wood chairs at home and make life easier for Bee and the kids. A bit of sponge rubber or a cushion underneath and they'd have padded seats. I felt a sort of good thing in my insides then when I thought how they'd like it.

103

The train wheels ground and clattered and settled into a steady beat and under cover of the noise I got my leather. There weren't many workers in the carriage by then, just that half dozen that gets a bit lonely or frightened that there's someone behind them. There was someone behind them—me, but when they peeped round I'd be looking out the window or something innocent and they'd turn front again. I've often thought, sitting behind people late at night in a train, how easy it would be to bash in the head in front of you. To test what it feels like, I've sometimes got to my feet and raised my arm, pretending it's holding a hammer or iron bar, and felt the exciting warm feeling inside that I'd actually have if I brought it down crash. Once I even got up behind a man, with something in my hand—it was a big steel bolt I found on the platform—and you should have seen the face on the man when he saw me in the window and turned round to check if his eyes were telling the truth. He leaped away and I got out at the next station before he could see the guard. No one would have believed him, anyway, he had glasses and looked like a loud-mouthed complainer, and I had a collar and tie and hair done nicely, and a pretty even sort of look on my face. I look very harmless at times like that, specially if I take care to walk in a nice neat manner.

I didn't bash any heads that night. I had nothing massive enough, anyway. What I did, though, was wreck a train.

It wasn't very wrecked, just eased off the rails. You have to pick a place that's not too far out in the open, where you can get under cover in case you have to run for it. I got off at the next station and out the back end and into the shadow of an overhead bridge. The way to do it, you can use all sorts of things you find by the lines—blue metal, fishplates, bolts—you build up two ramps to take the leading bogie on a gentle tangent away from the rails, just a skinny angle is all you need. It has to be packed down very tight.

The other way is to loosen the fishplates and lever the rail out of line; all the train does then is just drop a bit and plough up a few sleepers. I did the ramp bit. The end of the station was dark and no one saw me. A few of the passengers got a jolt when the front carriage lifted nicely and drifted into the space between two sets of lines, but as a crash it wasn't much. I blocked the up line for about three hours, that was all. You get a better kick out of things like that if there's blood. Or even hysterical screams. But the workers returning home from their work cages didn't have a yell in them. Some even got out and stumbled across country, you had to laugh to see them trying to keep vertical, you'd think they were blind.

As I say, it wasn't a great success, but it was something. How many people live and die and crawl down into the clay and never wreck a train? You'd think they'd all be going like mad to accumulate a past which is something to be proud of instead of just sneaking through every day with no skin off. That's it. That's all the house-owning job-captive wants; to get through to bedtime each day with no bruises and no bleeding. They're mad; the past is their only possession. Even I can see that.

*

A lot of people are going to be upset when they read this. I can hear them asking why I do these things, even though I've just told them. They can tell me books full of things I shouldn't do, but who's going to tell me what I ought to do? Who? Besides the ratbags?

You hear people talk about maturity. That's the end. Who wants it? A mature loaf of bread is ready for the slicer. A mature worker is already on the skids. Did I say everyone ought to be equal? Hell, I don't know what to think.

I gave away the thinking and got up for the night under a railway bridge down the line a bit. It was dry, and some warm air left over from daytime was trapped there. In the morning I thought I'd leave another little message for future archaeologists, so I lay on my back and drew on the underside of the concrete, which was only a foot above my face and had the prints of the timber forms on its skin, a cosy little picture of a train being derailed and a kid watching from up a tree. Someone in the future would think there had been a sort of guerilla war going on. I even put the date. No one in my time would ever see it, and there was something good about that. A storm blew up. You could hear it racing towards you making drums out of all the trees, until the first big drops stung you cold. I pulled my head in.

I couldn't help thinking of Bee, though, and all the nights she had to look after the kids herself, sitting up trying not to look at the television programmes, with a book in her soft lap because she wanted to keep up with what was going on in the world. And while I had her in my mind I could swear I heard the way her cups chimed when you tapped their thin lip edge, with the clear light of morning flooding the east window.

I had a good sleep there in the daytime, no one disturbed me. Milk shakes and fruit were my food that day. At night I had a high old time remembering.

I remember. That's enough to make anyone bored, reading it. But it doesn't bore me, and this is my story. If anyone doesn't want to read it, all they have to do is stop.

There is my first doorway, the first I slept in. I can see it now in the shadow in the main street of Tamworth where I ran away to when I was fourteen and sick of home. A dirty great copper woke me with his torch and sent me down under the bridge to sleep; there were branches there and you could make a mattress to kip on.

I didn't realise what a long job this book was going to be. Can't you write faster or something? Still, if it's going to be any good it'll take all we've got, I suppose. One thing at a time, from now on; I've spent sixteen and three-quarter years hopping from one thing to another; now's the time to settle down to one thing at a time, and this book is it.

Petersen, who met me on a railway station one morning, was tall as a pole with a pin-head. He was some sort of psychologist as well as a writer, and analysed me with tests down at the Red Cross, inkblot stuff, Rorschach, you know what it's like; I think that's a picture of two people dancing—that's very interesting, very few people see any violent movement, can you describe them more clearly—well, they're in evening clothes—that's amazing. That kind of stuff. One night he asked me what would I do if he suggested we lay down together in bed and that took me by surprise; maybe it was no wonder someone knifed him in China. He taught me a few things, though; I don't want to give the impression I'm not grateful.

When I got back I was so broke I had to sell my rifle to one of my brothers. It was new and cost twenty dollars then, so he gave me five and a lesson in business.

In the middle of my remembering I couldn't help wondering again—it happened every day, practically—wondering if my people had any idea what they were doing. When they got together, did they have a clue about what their offspring could turn into? Poor Ma, she had a terrible life. Yet maybe she was happy some of the nine months.

Getting back to going to bed with other blokes, like Petersen wanted, reminds me of three other times at Saratoga, Tascott and Marrickville. What was there about me that made these kids want to treat me like a girl? Is it because of that that I have got right away from going round with other kids and prefer to be a lone wolf? Maybe it's not only because the police have started their savage old policy of breaking up any gatherings, even two kids together. If I'd been the police I'd never have done that. Look at me. They'll never catch up with me; I have no other gutless kids to rat on me; to catch me they'd need a net like a mosquito net. Another thing, they'll never work out why I'm against them, so they'll never know how to go about catching me. They can never get at me, not the me inside. There's no such person. I'm convinced of it. A hundred kids like me, all working alone, and this sweet old society would be on its ear in a week.

I'll never forget running back from Lion Island, eight kids in a twelve foot boat, when the wind sprang up in the afternoon around four o'clock. Boy, that was when I decided never to work with other kids. You'd never believe how brave some of them were on dry land, there was Eddie; he'd walk up to any service station and get the till and shoot the Alsatian dog, but see him in that boat and you wouldn't give two bob for him. For a firm footing on a bit of rock he would have sold his mum and chopped his old man in little pieces with an axe, like he was always threatening to do. His old man was lame in one leg. We were only young, then. About the age when you sneak up to the lovers at Bobbin Head and creep up the rocks to watch them at their tricks. Too young to do it, though.

I'd never seen what my parents did together, so when I was old enough to start, myself, all I knew to do was the kissing I'd seen on the films and the tricks I'd seen on naughty photographs and on the sly in parks when the men and women didn't see you looking. When I was twelve, though, and the bigger kids let me come with them, I found out how easy it was. The girls were dying to be popular with us and the way to be popular was to be tough and to be in it. Just those two things. They didn't even have to look like girls.

The second movie I ever saw in my life was *Kidnapped*, and since I wasn't allowed to go to the pictures because of my old man's religion, and because it was such a long way away—I went to a school filming—I had to come out early. A little girl called Dot who used to watch us at cricket, came out at the same time and I sat with her all the way to Warrawee. Boy, if that'd been a year later, I'd have known

109

how to make sure she got home a different girl. As it was, all she wanted to talk about was cricket. She wanted a hero. She was too stupid to know that I never thought of cricket, ever, until I was down there on the pitch with a ball in my hand or two hands on a bat.

A sudden shadow slapped me across the face. Two kids had found me, under the bridge. They were on the run from their parents and they wanted a place to hide. When they saw me they wanted me to help. All they wanted was a boss. A leader. I tried to tell them the thing to do was to go alone, but they didn't know what I meant.

They were changing, while I talked to them, from people, that is humans like me, into things; I could just look at them and they turned into thick things like rocks and tree stumps, things not like me. You could bash them and they wouldn't be hurt. I did, and took the shillings they had in their pockets. They were too scared to dob me in to the police and their uniforms; they ran away very fast and left me to my thinking and my bridge.

My old man was tickled, it's the only time I recall him smiling, when I asked him why the breadman had a horse with lumpy veins. I still remember the varicose look of the horse in the shafts; I'd been used to seeing horses that were smooth and shiny, even if they were a bit on the ribby side. That was at Rosehill. Half a dozen house movings later, and with my first bird shot, I started on the bakers' horses and cows in the paddocks and the chinaman's pumpkins in the patch across the way. That was in Bay Road. The chinaman is gone; what were once his fields is now a park, with only grass growing.

That reminded me of another gun. I was coming home late to the house one night and this brother of mine—he's gone now—charged out with a twelve-gauge shotgun on full cock to blast Sexy Rexy. It's a wonder he didn't blast me when I grabbed the choked-down end, but at least Sexy Rexy went away without a large hole in him. They were both drunk, anyway, they probably wouldn't have noticed if they got shot, either of them.

When my ship comes in, she said—my auntie it was, on the front verandah of the old house in Bay Road one Sunday night around half-past eight—when my ship comes in, there were a lot of things going to happen then. They never happened. Her poor old ship was never sighted; it probably never sailed. Now she's on her uppers, back with another of my uncles, the one that handed me down his old watch when the old man died and told me to mend the verandah where the dry rot was eating it down; he's one of the brethren, too, you can't eat a biscuit or have a cup of tea with her even when he's out. Still, why should I mind if she's found a meal-ticket for the rest of her days? I hope she lives till she's a hundred, she's had it pretty tough; not as tough as Ma, but tough enough. Ma, she always wanted me to go back to being anything from two and a half to six, a little black boy that did everything she said. 'He used to be so nice and obliging.'

It was pretty quiet on the railway lines then; I went down to see if I could hear any trains coming, the metal was cool on my ear and all quiet. I climbed back up to the road this time and went for a run, about half a mile and back under the bridge, just in time to have myself a brightly

111

coloured dream about Bee. I didn't mean to have this dream, it just came, all I did was lie down and it dreamed itself into my head.

The first thing I saw was Bee in a wide white dress bordered with a fine blue, tied up to a fat gum tree, the one that grows in the middle of the track on the way to Lorna Pass. She had her two arms spread wide and her legs pulled apart and tied around the bottom of the tree. The next thing was someone tying her to the tree; his back was towards me, but he was young. The next thing was Bee being carried along the track to the tree. The next thing was Bee being knocked on the head, further along the track, and as she fell, she hit her elbow and the blood came. It was clear, shining blood.

The funny thing about the dream was that it was backwards. First she was tied up and last she was knocked over; at first I didn't see what was happening to her after she was tied up. Then after a while, when my mind had been going back over the same track a few times, I began to sort things out, and as I did, the dream got round into the right sequence. Until then, although I'd seen her scraped elbow in the last part of the dream, I hadn't seen any blood on her elbow in the first part. When my head got this right, I saw the dream right through from the beginning, and right past Bee being tied up with blood on her elbow, right through to seeing who it was that was blindfolding her and tearing her white dress off with the blue border, down to her pale blue panties and stiff white brassiere. She didn't have a really exceptional chest.

Why blindfold her? She must have seen the kid. But

no, perhaps she was really knocked out—yes, it would be better that way—she was knocked out right up to the time he blindfolded her, then she awoke while he stripped her. Yes, that would be better; kinder to Bee and better for me. It was me did it. You couldn't help guessing that, I reckon. Even in the dream I was a bit ashamed, but that added a sort of extra kick to the whole procedure.

You'd think I would have woken up hot from a dream like that, but in fact I was very cold indeed. I wished Stevo was there to tell me about the Chantic Bird. I would have listened. Honest. I wouldn't have bought him off with lollies or a bag of potato chips.

That dream must have got me. Who put me here? The bugger. I'd like to see him in my shoes. I have to admit I never thought I would be dreaming of doing things like that to Bee. I tried to put that sort of thing out of my head, by thinking more about the kids and the funny things they said.

Stevo was always talking about me getting little. I suppose I started it in the first place by telling him that when he was grown up I'd have to look up to him to see his face; I thought that was the best thing to tell him when he was always having to bend his neck back to look up at me, it might take the funny feeling out of his mouth at always being the small one. I wanted to stay friends with Stevo, and I reckoned the best sort of friends are sometimes stronger than each other and sometimes weaker than each other.

'When will I get little, boy?'

'You get little when your strength blows out.'

He even reckoned I'd be a baby again.

'When you're born I'll tie you up for fourteen days. When you're tiny I'll smack you.' I remember telling him that people got a bit shorter when they're old; that's where he must have got the tiny bit. And one day when we were in Robson the grocer's and they were giving away free samples of porridge he made us all laugh by suddenly yelling out at Robbo:

'Hey, Mister! I've got some porridge at home and I don't eat it—so I don't want this!' All the people in the shop smiled at Stevo—they always do. The only ones that don't appreciate him are relatives or neighbours with kids the same age, they find something wrong with everything he does right.

When he came into the room once and thought we were hugging and kissing—actually we were bending over near each other, Bee and I, tying up some parcels for their Christmas tree—he asked Bee what was the name for two people that loved each other. She said, Sweethearts, but he shook his head.

'I'll call you honey lovers. The other name sounded too sweet.' Boy, you can imagine the way I felt.

One day, after I'd done some prowling in Eastwood— a lot of these outer suburbs are good prowling places because in addition to having no regular police they often don't like to report anyone even if they see you; they have dignity, or something—I had to get home fairly smartly and I was hiding up in the ceiling so that if anyone came even Bee wouldn't know I was there and she wouldn't have to lie, I was lying on the sheet of hardboard I'd put down on one of the ceiling joists where the cross members met it

114

and when I got my breath back and the old ticker quieted down I had a listen to old Stevo.

'I think your friend Elaine has a rather attractive house,' he noted. What a way to talk! The kid was only six, after all.

'Their auntie says it's a bit on the cold side,' Bee put in. She often came home with a stiff back after sitting in her friend's kitchen, she told me once.

'It's a good house, if you run about a lot,' he amended.

'Are you going to play with your toys now?' she asked him. She probably wanted to get on with the dinner.

'I'll just bring my crane out,' he tailed off.

'Yes. Or else?' she prompted.

'Or else I won't bring my crane out.' She left him to it, and I agreed with her. Any kid that knew how to talk like that was OK. You wouldn't have to be watching after Stevo all the time.

I was just settling down on my stomach to have a bit of a sleep when something he said made me prick up my ears.

'Mummy, why do men like looking at ladies?'

'What men, sonny boy?'

'Men like Daddy.'

'Daddy? What ladies does he look at?'

'He looks at you.'

'Go on.'

'A lot. He looks at you a lot.'

'No one looks at ladies that do housework.'

'Daddy does. He must love you.'

I listened very hard to hear what she said to that. There wasn't a sound. I looked over to where the manhole cover was. No, it was on. There was no light coming up. Maybe she knew I was there. Maybe she was stuck for an answer. She used to stand a certain way when she looked at you. Her back foot was facing away but the front one was straight out, pointing. She was probably standing like that just then.

I waited there a long time, holding my breath mostly, but at last she went on with getting the food ready, and not saying a word. I settled my ribs down to the hardboard again and my head on one side and got ready for a sleep. But what did I get in my head but the memory of my last visit to my old man at Randwick TB hospital. There were gallant diggers, old soldiers they call them, making death noises to imitate my old man, who had just started to make his first few. The way he died, your breath gets caught somehow on the instroke, and when something inside you is calling out for breath and your chest tries to draw it in, there is some other thing inside you that turns the sound of the in-breath into a very loud groan.

With my young brother it was different. He groaned on the outstroke and made no sound on the instroke. I listened for two hours and his in-breath was quiet, not a rattle of any sort. But the out-breath was a groan, only a light one as if he was very sorry for something. Now that they're dead, and Ma too, they've become a sort of conscience to me. A pretty weak old conscience, I know, but still a sort of one.

Anyway, back to the old man. Those groans were very loud, and so were the imitations the other old soldiers made. You see, I knew what they were doing, because only three weeks before I heard them doing the same thing and he told me they were making a joke out of old Clarrie Rees who

116

was taking about a week to die. He heard the first few and stopped making his noise. But when I came back later, the last night it turned out to be, and slept on the billiard table, with the cat on the floor that the nurse said was riddled with TB, the old man was in full blast. He sure made a noise leaving this world. I must have fallen asleep at the time he actually snuffed it. Before I left I hoisted a metal pan out of the window far enough to bang against the next ward. It was dark, the walls were fibro. The night nurse jumped up and raced outside and while she was out I clobbered the six gallant old diggers that had done the mocking bird calls, with the thick end of a billiard cue. I brought Ma back in the morning, much use that was; she didn't even insist on viewing the body. The nurse sort of hinted that the old man was in a mess, and I would have liked to see him—he was my old man after all—but she said no. I had on a collar and tie and my hair nicely done, to keep suspicion off me, so I couldn't spoil the image by demanding to see Dad or threatening to wreck the joint. Could I? But you don't really know there's anyone in those coffins.

I was still feeling mad about the death-house for old diggers, when I heard a noise that reminded me I was back under a railway bridge and when I opened my eyes, there it was, daytime. An old dirty engine was in the station and a railway fettler was tramping off the end of the station towards me with a thick metal tool to tap the rails and the spikes that held the rails down. He found a few loosened ones and bashed them back down into place. For some reason I felt I had to get out of there. I felt he was after me. It must have been the early morning that made me come over all guilty. He found a few more loose spikes and knocked them back where they belonged, in line with the rest. Next it would be my turn.

I suppose he was only doing his job, finding the ones out of place. For a good railway you need not only a good engine, but good rails to carry it. For some reason I wondered why he didn't tap the wheels of the engine to see if they were safe or not.

1 0
CEILING

Stevo used to say 'Tampoo' for thank you. Chris said 'Tattoo' for thank you. That went over and over in my head all the way back home. I was still hanging on, in my head, to the sound of the kids' voices as they said Thank you, when I got up in the ceiling, took my coat off and got down on my sheet of hardboard. I don't know how long it was, but I woke hearing Bee say to Chris, 'Ah-ah! Chris. What you doing?'

'I not Chris,' said Chris. I nearly laughed out loud. She would be able to get away with what she liked when she was a big girl. For some reason I felt glad. It seemed to me then that it was important for girls to be able to do what they liked with the world.

When she went to sleep around eleven, there was an eye watching her in the cot. Later, when she woke up and

119

when I must have next woken up, there was an eye watching her, with glasses. She said this with a new sort of concern. The glasses were an added menace. When she helped Bee with the washing up and Bee told her to mind how slippery the dishes were—Bee used a detergent I got straight from an oil company, it wasn't broken down—and she dropped a couple, she got in first to Bee with,

'Little children like me don't have any sense what their mothers tell them to do.'

I was watching down through a crack in the ceiling then, and I saw Bee watching her with tears in her eyes. I went back and lay down again, I didn't want to see any emotional women putting on a turn.

Stevo wasn't in my line of sight and I started to wonder what had happened to him. I thought I'd better go down and offer to listen to his story of the Chantic Bird again to make him happy, but from what Bee said I found Stevo was sick. So that was that. No story.

There's strength in the air, just above your head, if you can reach it. You only need the right knack of doing it. Strength to get through and above your own troublesome self, strength to make your chest puff up and make you equal to the opposition in whatever fight you're in. I had my ear to the main roof beam at that moment and I swear I heard a tuneful humming from the body of the house, a sort of noise that made all the sour things inside you curl up and die, and all the good healthy things revive that don't normally have much of a chance.

*

120

Bee went in to see how Stevo was getting on, I heard them, but you can't see them from where I was in the ceiling. She told him the news about Elaine moving, and how she couldn't find a house they wanted round about.

'Well, if they can't find a house in this neighbourhood, why don't they try another neighbourhood,' suggested Stevo, and the joke was, that Bee said about them not being able to find a house handy because she wanted to introduce tactfully the idea of his friends moving away, but she found he was quite prepared for whatever happened.

'Perhaps we could help them, by looking up some houses for sale,' helped Bee.

'I was just thinking. There are lots of fine houses. I read it in the *Herald*.' Stevo surprised her. She got so emotional about Stevo being awake up to what was going on, plus his being sick, that she covered him over with hearty kisses. I wish I'd been sick enough for them.

But Stevo was used to that sort of treatment.

'Just give me a dry one,' he pleaded. 'Try not to get upcited when you're kissing me.'

She was so worked up that she started to get wet around the eyes again, then with a lot of drops in her eyes she laughed.

'What's so funny?' he demanded aggressively.

'I don't know,' she said, to head him off. She fished around in her things and got them all lollies, to take their attention away from the wetness around her eyes.

'Ah,' put in Stevo, 'I like lollies, because I can relax with them.'

121

I suppose it was reaction, but Bee started to get a little sharp with them after she had cried over them. She ordered them about a bit.

'Some day I'm going to break your heart,' promised Stevo. He wasn't sure what was going on inside her; it was his way of saying she should ease up.

I lay back on the hardboard, trying to put my thoughts in some sort of order. But all I could do was bring back to mind Stevo's excited cry last Christmas, 'Look at all the presents I've got! Everyone must be mad about me!'

They were only ordinary presents, but there were a couple of dozen of them from all the people he knew and he thought he was made.

Why should I suddenly remember the way everyone looked at me when Stevo had to go back to the hospital every day for his dressing on the leg I burned? Why should it come back to smash me down every time I wasn't expecting it?

Was it something I had got from my parents? Was it a sign there was something corrupt in my parents? No. My parents weren't corrupt, they weren't anything. It was the same with me. I knew I was more than equal to most of the kids I ever knew, but there was no place for me. There was no actual function, no legal function, that would fit me.

The wind in the wires outside moaned and it was the sound I should have made. I couldn't stand the thoughts that crowded into my head and spilled over on my tongue so that I found myself talking aloud. I got out and went back to the city and set fire to a city fire station while all the men were in bed—the night shift is provided with bunks—then another fire in an Arcade off Elizabeth Street. I knew that if there were two fires in the city at the same time there were not enough engines to put them out. They were still on water instead of dry powder, so I had the jump on them. Besides, their water pressure couldn't get up above a hundred and twenty. I knew private firms that had up to two hundred and fifty pounds pressure and I'd seen some of the fires they couldn't put out, so I was sure the poor old under-equipped brigades wouldn't be able to handle what I'd set them.

I watched from fifty yards. I noticed a man watching me and I wasn't sure what expressions I'd had on my face while he was watching, so I didn't know what he thought about me.

Presently he came over and asked me to help him park his caravan. He was an interesting case; he might have been a perve or a copper's nark, or an ordinary citizen, but I wasn't in a position to judge. I cleared out. The sort of face he had and the way he stood reminded me of uniforms.

11
STAGE

'Look at the mountain, singing like a bird.' I was keeping away from home, to give them a rest from me. 'A sea breeze has come down.' I'll never forget that. I had borrowed one of the cars at the station quite early one morning, just after the worker who drove it got on his train to Sydney, and I took the kids out for a drive to the beach. And Bee. I don't know what Stevo had been reading—he was like me, he started reading when he was young—but whatever it was, it had made him a poet. Those were his own, exact words. I didn't make them up just so someone would say how clever he was. If anyone wants to say how clever he is, they can go right ahead and say it. He is. I looked up where he pointed, and sure enough, all I could see was hills above us. It was a fine day all right, but the only birds I saw were birds, not mountains. I didn't hear any singing. He remarked that a

124

sea breeze had come down when we were on the beach and he was standing there wet, looking back at the dry sand and the hills beyond the traffic and the shops.

I remembered all this while I was camped under the stage of the local picture show. Television had white-anted their audiences, and they had to use the place for other things besides films, since they couldn't keep going all week on the leftovers from the big distributors. I knew all that because I asked the man once why we didn't get the new films for months. That was why some of the time, when churches, for instance, had a party or a play or a meeting on, I'd be looking up holy legs from my crack in the cypress. On movie nights, I had a view of the whole stage, but it was from one side and the screen, instead of being a rectangle, was a very squashed parallelogram and the people were wafer thin. You expected them to peel off the white back cloth any minute. And when they walked, it was a nightmare. Only their voices came loudly to me below.

The whole point of this is that I was still held prisoner by my habit of getting away from the family, then remembering them and going over their good points at a safe distance. I knew that well enough, there was no need to kid my own self.

The second day I was there I had this new sort of dream. You know how I often have coloured dreams, even if they're only green and brown dreams like the one where I was shot in the head. Well, this was a one-colour dream, the colour stone. But there were stone colours of all sorts, within what you could call recognisable stone colours, even to the grey weathered look you get in the bush rocks, and the purple patches of sandstone when you split it.

I was a mountain. A stone hill. Not like Ayer's Rock; I was steeper, fiercer. Naturally. I was a mountain and people were chipping away at me. That's right, chipping. You know how it is when the doctor puts some snow on your back and cuts out a cyst, or lances a boil—I mean the times when the anaesthetic actually takes and you feel nothing—well, that's how it was. You could hear the operation, but feel only pressure, not pain. There were people all over me, chipping and napping away with hammers and picks and chisels. I don't know why; I couldn't see what they were doing with my pieces, but from the look of the people, they were carting bits of me away to make into statues and sculptures. You know, 'The Unknown Factory Prisoner' with round fat bits of stone instead of the cyclone netting and barbed wire like on real factories. There were even a few chisellers making faces out of me, faces of other men. I guess you could call them famous faces, but I wouldn't. I don't recognise famous, or well-known, or rich, or anything that isn't ordinary.

Hacking me to make other men's faces! I wouldn't be a block for people to carve and shape up into other shapes. They weren't going to make me into something else! So what I did, I split. If there was any shaping to do, I'd do it. I left off dreaming then, probably because I didn't like the idea of having got smaller, that is, broken into smaller pieces. They left, then, the ones who weren't destroyed in the crash. In a week, though, they'd forgotten, as if the passing of a lump of time meant that I was any safer for them to climb on. When they came back, I landslid some surface rock on them, and since they couldn't get on me any more, they put up a sign at my bottom, TRESPASSING PROHIBITED.

I was lucky they didn't do the usual thing and blast me, doing the very thing I threatened them with. It amazed me that they didn't get the message; all they had to do was associate my splitting with their being on me, and my not splitting with their not being on me. After that, all they had to do was keep off my back. One warning ought to be sufficient to the reasonable ones. But I don't think there were any.

Going back that day in the car Stevo was so happy—he still had his trunks on; you couldn't get them off him—that in the middle of singing, he suddenly burst out, 'I'm a silver-winged robin!' I sneaked a look at Bee in the driving mirror to see the nice expression on her face. I ought to explain that she liked to sit in the back seat; she said it was luxury, like having a chauffeur. What it was, though, she wanted to keep me away. By keeping herself away from me, she thought she could take my mind off things.

Under the footlights, I was in a different world. It was as if there was no world there, and I had to import one from outside or conjure one up by looking through a crack up into someone else's world.

I'll tell you the most surprising thing. I wondered what I'd struck on picture nights. There were two paths down opposite sides of the theatre building, going to the back and the toilets. I knew what kids said to one another, so I got across the other side and listened to the women. I wish I'd had some witnesses. You wouldn't believe the filth they go on with when they're together. Still, I'm used to what men say. You have to laugh, though, when you think of it. There's a stream of men on one side of the building going on with the usual, and a stream of women on the other side, going on with their usual, then they turn, both streams, and come back. As soon as the streams get together, the filth stops and they talk about the picture, the car, the kids or the weekend, anything but what they most enjoy talking about.

It was pretty dark under the stage and some days I had to rely on the factory whistles to remind me to get out and grab some food. The best thing I thought of to scare the people that had meetings there was hiding the skin of a little green tree snake under the seat of a chair and dropping it when they were halfway through and fed up, and pulling it with brown cotton about two feet towards my little knothole. You can only do that sort of thing for a short distance if you have to use cotton, if you make it any longer they get on to the cotton.

When Stevo used to try to explain something to me and I'd pretend not to understand what he was describing—I only did it so he would get the idea of searching his head for words instead of using the first ones that occurred to him, that might be right and might not be—and when he couldn't make me see he'd say, 'You only see what you're looking at, Daddy.' Well, that was the same with those people. All they could see was the skin of the snake, they didn't look any further for the cotton. For that trick you have to dry the snake out and draw him, then work the skin with oil. Don't usc motor oil, it makes the skin brittle. Then you don't quite fill it with dry sand. If you fill it, it won't wriggle.

The church turnouts were the funniest, next to the Parents and Citizens who had committees to get money for the state schools. The mothers and fathers of the local schoolkids weren't really interested in what happened inside the classrooms. If I was a mother or father, I would be, because it's there the kids soak up a lot of prejudice from some unhappy teacher, and besides that, they're taught things that don't quite go down in the rest of the community. Like patriotism, for instance. What Australian is patriotic? What is there to be patriotic about? Yet you ought to hear the flag stuff and the British Empah jazz. It's watered down a bit now, but it's still mostly the same stuff. And what do they teach you about the Factories and Shops Regulations? Or the Crimes Act? Kids are let loose now and they don't know what not to do. In the olden days it was different, you had principles. But there's no principles now, no one's honest, no one's generous, no one cares a damn what happens to the next person. Look at me.

I shouldn't pretend they're worse than I am, though. I remember how I used to get into the cricket team when I was at school; I might have got five for none and all that when I did get in, but I never missed picking the longest straw, and if it was a case of picking out the bit of paper with your name on it, all you had to have was a memory for the size of the paper.

Remembering that, I felt pretty young, I can tell you. Most of the time I forget those sort of things, they're not really very bad. As a matter of fact, they're not bad enough, and that is why they embarrass me. Old time seems to fly away very fast at times, and every time he flaps his wings he smacks you in the mouth.

Stevo said once, 'Did you dress Daddy when he was a little boy?' to Bee. That made me feel about as young. But when Bee answered, I was in another world. She only said a few ordinary words. 'No, darling boy,' she said. 'He had his own Mummy to do that for him.' The words, though, sort of dropped very light from her lips, but didn't fall just anywhere like other people's words. Hers floated. They floated right into you, you could almost hear the tiny vibrations in your bones and veins.

I thought mostly about Bee for the next few days and I reckon I forgot to go out to raid the supermarket at Penno. I used to take advantage of the cheating the food people used to do. You know the packets of breakfast foods or any other packets, they are never filled up. If you slit a cornflakes packet in a special way and press down the flakes to about an inch off the bottom of the packet, you can stuff it with all sorts of other things, as long as you insulate the tins with something that will deaden the noise. And for the price of cornflakes you can have dollars' worth of food. But if you try it, don't let the girl on the desk pick it up. They're supposed to, I know, but if you only get a few things they can add up easy without picking them up, and they like you to wrap them yourselves if they can get you to. I was always obliging like that.

Anyway, I got no food. I was thinking. Next thing it was Saturday and the films were on, and the usual mucking up.

I'll tell you what, I was so quiet inside from thinking of Bee that I got a hankering to get into the movies to join in with the other kids rolling bottles down the aisles or even, if the kids in front were cheeky, even getting rid of empties by hurling them. That was a pretty cruel game, I know, someone was always getting hurt. You had to keep your eyes open to make sure it wasn't you.

Like Stevo said, 'Every time you want to do something, you do it.' He knew. I paid and went in and next thing I felt a hand on my shoulder. I was in a seat, so it wasn't a queer. What it was, a kid wanted to rest his catapult on my shoulder while he took aim at someone up front. I was glad I came. It was nice to be able to get back into the ways I liked. I used to do that myself when I was a kid.

Where we had it over the old people, we never used to worry about dignity. I've thought a lot about it, because on the face of it, they ought to be able to beat us. But to get at us, they have to drop this business of walking tall and upstanding, walking and speaking nicely and slowly, and everything that adds up to the word dignity. They have to come down to our level to do any good. They have to be able to nick over a fence or down a pipe, up a tree or through a house and out the back. You can't wear good suits or smoke pipes and do those things, so we had them beat. But the funny thing was, instead of them copying us and being able to do the things we did, they kept as they were and wondered why we didn't copy them! Hell, who wants to look like an old man, all square and thick and closed up like a public building?

131

And the ones that tried to be like us and made a mess of it were the worst. As soon as we got out a new way of talking, to get away from their ways, they started to pound our words to death. Until we stopped using them. Then they were left dribbling the old-words and wondering what to say next, while we imported a new style.

My mind. At the back of my mind I have a feeling that there is something I'm going to do. Why do I say the back of my mind? All I know is I can't quite get at this thought, it doesn't seem to want me to grab it. Is it that I am going to kill someone? Is it something I have to do? Or want to do?

I woke up from thinking to hear the sound of a man's hand on a shirt. Rub your shirt with your hand and you'll see what I mean. There were people coming in for a meeting, and shortly I found myself again looking up holy legs from under the platform. The women had no lipstick on and I thought straight away of Plymouth Rocks and the old man giving up the insurance and going broke and trying the rest of his life to give up smoking because it was sinful, but drinking wasn't and he didn't like the taste of beer anyway and couldn't afford anything dearer. When I was a kid I used to practise holding my breath in their meetings, they had a beaut electric clock on the wall at Beecroft, and I got up to two minutes. I was about twelve then, only a kid. The idea was you had to hold it as long as you could, but you couldn't let it out noisily, everything had to be quiet. No matter what you let go there, you had to be quiet. They

132

didn't even like you turning the pages of your hymn book and making a noise.

We often had Sunday dinner with the biscuit kings or the meat kings, and boy, did we eat, my brother and me.

They certainly gave us a lesson in comfort. I often thought, as we tucked into the roast pork or the mountains of delicious fresh cream, how funny it was that most other religions sort of praised poverty and plain living while this mob had never heard of it. When we got home from their two-storey houses on Sunday night we always found that our own little fibro wreck of a house had shrunk to the size of a kid's play-shack, the sort you see balanced crazily in the fork of a tree.

I got out into the fresh air again and straightened up and walked and walked, and the first thing that hit me was a terrific big white wave. Of cheerfulness. I was swamped in a heap of bright feelings, tossing over and over, I felt I was being dumped in the surf, and the joy of the world was getting up my nose and suffocating me. I must have rolled a bit as I walked, because some people tch-tched as I staggered by, drowning. I not only must have rolled, I must have looked very harmless at that time, because people don't usually make any remarks when I pass. When I got my breath after a struggle, my chest took great swells of air and I felt my eyes bright and hardening and almost pushing out of my head, I felt so well.

It faded quickly, and all I was left with was sore eyes. My eyes always get gritty and sore and need lubrication, when I have an emotional attack like that. Or even when

I drink too much and talk and shout at the same time. It was bad luck for me, though, that I'd been so high a few minutes before, because after that I sank down very bad. I remember thinking to myself, perhaps this isn't life at all, yet. Maybe it's a sort of pre-life, a foyer, a vestibule, an ante-chamber of life and I'm due to get to live sometime later. But life isn't around you, on this planet. Practically everything around you is dead; you have to move things yourself and be the only life there is. Life is buried in us and you sometimes have to dig it out.

I felt so crook about this, that a few tears came into my eyes at the misery of it. It was just as well, too. The salt water made my eyes feel fine and pretty soon I cheered up, knowing that I could still rise above these silly feelings, I could still tread on them when I wanted to.

I switched my head over from thinking of myself to thinking of Stevo; that always made me forget everything.

When I had them out for another day not long ago, he suddenly cried out in the car, bouncing up and down in his seat, 'The bindies are hot with joy!' That's exactly what he said. I put it down in pencil on the paint of the dashboard of the car I'd borrowed. I didn't even know what it meant.

'Did you get a load of that?' I yelled to Bee, in the back seat.

'What do you mean, boy?' she asked him.

'They make you go Yow!' he bubbled. That was all he would say. You couldn't help being proud of a kid who could say things like that. And later, when I overtook a trailer with a light load trying to keep me behind him, he said, 'Some drivers look away or look ahead. And some put their eyes at ya!'

The way he stared round at them it was no wonder. But it was a pity if they couldn't take a little kid staring. I'd never thought of it before, but I guess there wasn't much for a kid to do in a car between stops. The next thing I remember, he was fiddling with his hat. You had to ask a kid like that what he was doing, if only on the offchance of hearing some brand new idea, from wherever it is they come from just before they're born.

'I have to have the brim of my hat up, so the other drivers can see my eyes talking to them.' I reckon if I'd ever said things like that when I was a kid, my parents would have stayed alive instead of dipping out, just to hear more. All the rest I remember of that trip is the way Stevo called the television cartoons Dopeys and Chris called them Popeyes. Even if you took them a hundred miles away, their minds were never far away from home.

Without thinking about it I found that I'd walked home. The house watched me, I could feel its eyes following me. The trees listened. Each empty paddock had the look of a minefield.

I was rubbering round the verandah, the way I do, when I heard Stevo. They never actually expected me, but they were always ready for me when I got there, no matter when.

'We won't tell Daddy there's no cake for him, 'cause that will unhappy him. We'll just let him see for himself.' I had missed dinner. I never said anything, but there was an arrangement that if I got there in time I ate; if not, I went without. It wasn't dark, anyway, I could eat later.

Instead of eating, Stevo started again on the story of the Chantic Bird. But he only got up to the part where the Chantic Bird's song was like the tinkling of glass bells, and he broke off to run outside and kick a ball, only it wasn't a ball. I watched him kick an old fruit tin around and when I looked at Bee, I could see she was anxious. It only took me about half an hour to see why. Stevo was hurting his shoes and he probably only had the pair he had on. I was disappointed he hadn't carried on with the story, I had come to expect it, and what with that and the thought of his shoes, I felt very sorry for the poor little kid and raced out to roll a drunk. I had to wait a bit more for it to get dark, then I got on to old man Keble coming down the hill from the Hampden. I bowled him and rolled him and went right back home and made out I'd forgotten to give her the money before, and gave her the old drunk's donation. Actually, that wasn't all. The money smelt so much of beer, I had to rub some of her fancy soap on it so she wouldn't smell it.

I hung round a bit, then I decided to go back to the theatre. On the way I thought of my brother, the one that died, and how when he was in that beautiful old Catholic hospital he was put next to a criminal. This man was going to bottle him with a lemonade bottle, he reckoned. I saw the sisters and made sure a cop was there by his bed twenty-four hours a day, but my brother wasn't happy until he got into another ward. They put him out on a verandah because they knew you thought things were going good if you were outside. He was dying, of course, but no one was supposed to tell him. I'd want them to tell me, it was too much like a dog

136

dying, the way he went. But the thing that hits you between the eyes is that no matter what time of day or night it is, something's killing something. The hawks overhead and the sparrows looking nervously over their shoulders, the mice darting, the owls calling, the birds after the butterflies, the killing doesn't stop. With my brother it was a tiny germ in his blood.

All of a sudden I heard something, a stiff curtain on rings slid back. For a moment I thought I was back in the theatre and I got a cold feeling in the back of my head. Then I realised the sound was only in my head after all; it was the sound the curtain made round my brother's bed when he had an attack and the blood supply to his brain was interrupted.

I waited around outside the theatre and just when I was about to go in, a man and a woman appeared and went in. Everywhere I went there were people following me, or if not following me, then blocking me. I hopped on the next train out of there and the first thing I did when I got off at Penno was to run up the steep cutting as fast as I could.

You've got to watch the citizens. They'll call copper if you look sideways at them. What it was, I must have collapsed somewhere. You couldn't tell the coppers from the meat-wagon men from where I was on the ground; their legs were all the same and they were too close to my head.

If there was anything funny that night, it was the sound, in the ambulance, of Stevo's voice talking to Bee.

He spoke, 'Come on, wake yourself up. Make a fuss! I'll help you wash up—poor old thing!' Don't get me wrong, he wasn't really there with me, that was what he said to Bee after they had heard that I was in hospital. I was seeing it in my head, and I hoped that when it happened it would be the way I imagined it, because it was a good feeling to think Bee was worried. When thoughts like that hit you, you have to laugh. There I was, the sort of human that goes round making a bump and smash wherever I could, and getting away with it, and underneath the fine, proud actions of bashing and stealing and assaulting I was hoping a sixteen-year-old girl was crying and upset over me. They left a man in a blue uniform with me in the back of the ambulance, and when he heard me laughing he leaned forward to see if I was laughing at him, and he was ready to land me one, don't you worry, and I was glad again when I saw that, because I was right—I had always been right—they were exactly the same sort as me; they'd smash a young kid lying down in an ambulance without a thought. If no one was there to see. You can't imagine how pleased I was with that. They're the same sort as me, don't you worry about that, so don't get mixed up with them, and if one day one of them is in a crappy mood and you're waiting on a corner for someone after dark at night and he tells you to move on; you just move on and don't argue. Or else. He had a voice like a soft-nose bullet; you thought how round and cheerful they felt in your hand, but they thumped home hard.

He didn't smash me one, though. I let my head go limp and rolled it to one side towards him. If I'd flopped the other side he might have thought I was being smart, dodging the punch I expected. I might have copped it, that way. Instead, with my head flopped near him, he thought I'd collapsed again and got the driver to go faster. I wanted to get them to turn on the siren and I was nearly going to ask them, but they did anyway. They usually do if they get irritated and what got them irritated was going along nice and steady and then being asked to step on it. Just for the sake of some rotten little b, which was what they called me when I was coming round. I heard them say it. And when there was no one round that wasn't in their little club.

Did you ever try my little trick on a doctor? When he's taking your pulse, you relax, breathe in deep, then breathe out very hard. Your pulse slows down, not gradually, but it sort of pauses then gives a big thump and then none for a little time. It gets back a bit faster after that, then it's time for another breath out. It will thump again after a nice pause. The doctor will look at you—they're very careful about getting tricked, and also, if there's something the matter with you and they're the only ones that know, they like to get a look at your face; I think it gives them a lift to know you're clapped out and you don't know it, especially if they've got another thirty years to go. When he looks at you, you're on your own. I was all right, I know how to look innocent. If you're not used to it, look out the window or pretend you're having trouble with your eyes. Something. They never believe anyone else can keep track of a couple of things at a time; if you're squinting, they'll never believe you could be putting one over at the same time.

There's another thing, if you can manage it. You think of something that always frightens you, and your ticker will go faster. If you do that after you've been slowing it down, you'll have him shake his head and peer at you. That's the time to be looking out the window. I used to think of a football team of legs with blue and white socks, running out onto the field. Remember the nervous feeling you have before a game? Well, those legs reminded my heart of that feeling and it beat faster.

Apart from anything being wrong, I'm fine. The bed is good and hard; I'm only comfortable on a hard bed, or the floor or a rock or a grating or something like that. I can't say actually comfortable, but I feel better inside when I'm living hard. It's as if I'm not asking any favours.

Bee and the kids came to visit me. Littlies are not supposed to come in; their germs are too strong for grown-ups. But I got them to go round to the other entrance—it was at Hornsby—not the entrance the visitors use, and anyone who saw them then thought they'd been allowed in at the other end, and no one stopped them. Chris was coming on about that time; she started climbing up some oxygen bottles onto a shelf; she wanted to sit there, she was too short to see me properly from the wooden floor.

Bee commanded, 'You can't get up there, Chris!'

'Yes I can,' said Chris. 'You know me.' That cheered me up. The doctors had started going over me and letting the young learning doctors have a go at me. You're in for that in the public ward. The young ones were very taken with some flat brown marks on my legs and arms; from the way they looked you'd have thought they were the blunt tentacles of cancer coming up to the surface for oxygen. For all I know they might have been.

Bee got Chris down, anyway, and that made her yell. It was good to hear a little kid yell with something besides the agonies.

Stevo said, 'Be quiet for a minute Chris! Mum, why do ladies scream?' Chris sneaked away to look at the television set in the ward and came back delighted. Someone gave her some lollies to go away. We asked her what she saw and she said a nice girl on the television with her arms wrapped round a man.

'I think she loves her daddy,' she explained. We made her give some of the free lollies to Stevo. 'Lollies make me strong, don't they?' he reminded us. To Bee he said, 'Why did you say before I can't have chips? Because they give me bad breath?' Bee was cornered there, but she didn't have to answer. He knew when he'd won, he didn't have to hear her admit it.

I started to feel stronger with Bee and the kids about and it wasn't long before I started to think to myself, Why should I stay still for these people in white coats to prod me and look in everywhere in me and ask me questions and expect me to do what they said and stay here until they let me go? Why should they have any power over me at all? Just because of words written on pieces of paper? That was all that made them official. Take away the bits of paper and what were they?

'Now hear this,' was Stevo's command. He saw me drifting off on my own wavelength and he wanted me back.

'Now hear what?' I said. He got confidential.

'I like little girls.'

'Which little girls?'

'Ones at school and new ones I meet.' Bee looked pretty depressed, but she smiled at that.

'Why don't you have mummies at school?' he asked.

'I don't think they'd get much work done. Mummies have a pretty easy time,' I reckoned. Bee didn't come in.

'It's a possibility,' he commented.

'Why don't you start telling Daddy more of your story?' Bee questioned. Daddy. Stevo didn't look too happy.

'Daddy's sick.'

He started then, but all the time he spoke he was looking out the window and I could see he wasn't going to get very far. I'll tell you what, he only got as far as last time. He stopped almost the same place as before. One minute he was talking about the song like glass bells and the tears in the King's eyes and the silk ropes on the Bird's feet, and the next he was outside running over to a culvert in the hospital yard down near the paddock with the horse. He was digging with a stick and later he brought back some very white clay to take to school and make little figures.

Bee didn't seem to mind him running off and forgetting the story, but I reckon she knew her own mind. It was more important for me to give the kid an ear than for him to be made to stick there and talk when he didn't want to.

Chris was showing a lot more life. She got up to Stevo's little lolly box of treasures that Bee carried in her brown bag and took out his cards that he saved out of the cornflakes packets.

Bee said, 'They're Stevo's cards.'

'Will he hit me?'

'He might.'

'I don't care. I'll cry later.' What a kid. I was so happy, I knew she was going to be as big a character as Stevo. The only one left now was Allie; I didn't know what she would turn out to be, but she was only young.

Bee gave me a folded-up paper from Stevo. Since it was folded he called it a book. There were coloured-in drawings on it, but I'll only tell you what he wrote.

143

Mrs Hen layed an egg down by the road
side. Mr Dog said Why did you. I didn't have
a home. I'll build you a home. No, no.
But it was a golden egg.

Bee explained that the story was meant to cheer me up
while I was sick.

Bee went shortly after and the kids waved at the door
and that left me with only me to talk to. Almost everyone
around was dying. There were other kids there, mostly out
of car crashes, with broken this and that, but they weren't
the sort of kids you'd be breaking your neck to talk to. They
were proud of their head-on crashes, not ashamed of their
stupid reflexes, and they mostly had about fifteen thousand
other smashes to talk about. You'd think if they had one
prang that would be the last, they'd at least go to a car club
and learn to read the road conditions by the seat of their
pants, or something. Or else not talk about it.

If I was a big sort of thing watching the world, I'd have
a big rubber ready and I'd rub out all the nasty ones in the
world and the stupid ones.

The trouble is, I can see that even nice people have nasty
kids, and there'd soon be just as many nasty ones to rub out.

When I got up, I'd only been in bed a few days, but just the
same I was wobbly on my feet. It was so hard to get any
pace up that when I walked out onto the verandah of the
kids' ward—there were no nurses around, I could be doing
all sorts of things for all they cared—when I swayed out in
the middle of a crowd of kids I nearly got included in their

game. It was only a very simple game, I could probably have done it first go. But there was something about the feeling of nearly being a kid again that I didn't take any reprisals against them when I got shoved round a bit.

There was excitement that same day. One of the older kids was in a very filthy mood and a lot of the younger ones were playing near the toilets and one must have had his finger round the corner of the door jamb, because when this kid slammed the door in his bad mood, the edge of the door took off the top joint of the kid's finger. Some people just can't look after themselves. I wouldn't leave a finger in a place like that even if there was no one around. The kid was yelling very loud, much louder than when he was playing and the others were gathered round him in a circle looking at the stump; I saw the finger-bit on the floor and picked it up and gave it to one of the kid's friends and she tormented him with the sight of it and when the nurses came and the sister, she hid the piece and showed her parents that night. They didn't show proper appreciation so she put it in a match-box and sold it to one of the others for half a dollar and a bar of coconut rough.

I had a rest on my bed after about twenty minutes, whatever was the matter with me left me pretty tired. It was no use asking the doctors; they liked to be one up, they wouldn't tell me what was the matter or what they were looking for. If I'd had a few quid it would have been different, but when you're in a public ward you take what they dish out.

Another brother of mine had spent a lot of time in hospital, I remember while he was in once and nearly dead

145

I sort of stole his mate and that left him with no one to visit him. Why was I always doing bad things like that? The brother that died, he was taken in with bad pains to the very same ward I was in, only a year ago, but the doctor must have been a nut, he opened him up with a vertical cut and all that was wrong was appendix. You'd think they would have found the leukaemia in his blood then, but it's hard to spot if they don't even take blood tests.

Next time I got up I felt a bit better; there was a lot of fun to be had with the stray dogs that used to come in the park at the back of the hospital. They'd get some scraps here and there and I used to get some goolies ready, then scare them, and as they ran away, usually in a wide circle ready to come in the grounds again, I'd toss a rock high up in the air away on before the dog. With good aim, you'd see the rock high in the air, and the dog running along underneath in a straight line. The curve of the rock would come down to intersect the straight line. It was hard to actually hit a dog like that, but if you landed one just before or just behind, you'd get a result. And if you had a bad shot and went to one side of the dog, you'd have a fair chance of seeing him side-slip on his neck. They're easily startled.

The other patients used to get a bit disturbed, most of them were animal-lovers. They hated other humans. They'd nuzzle any old dog, but would they nuzzle any old stranger? No, sir. Once there was a beautiful shot going begging and I ran out to grab a rock. But I'd been sitting down for hours and I ran out very fast, without taking any breaths beforehand. After forty yards I had to stop, hunched over. My ticker wouldn't go. Then with a big effort, it gave a great thump as if it was blowing up a balloon with not enough air. For a while, although I was breathing, my chest felt as if I wasn't. I felt as you feel when you hold your breath, starved of air. Even though I was breathing. It's a wonder I'm still alive. It was easier when I hunched over, if I tried to straighten up I felt bad still.

What with all that, I had to think up something to show the world I was still there. They have ramps at both ends of that hospital; one down to the entrance, from the wards, and the other right through the other end to the theatre. Both ramps might have people on them at visiting, so I waited until after.

From the servery the stainless steel trolleys are wheeled out into the big corridor to wait for someone to take them round the wards. I detached one and took it to the top of the western ramp. You should have seen it sail down that covered porch. The rubber wheels were a big help and the weight of the plates on top and the food underneath. Lucky the front door was propped open—they have no air conditioning—for although the thing lost a few dinners going down the front steps, it kept most of the plates and knives and forks until it went off the gutter out front. If I was an engineer I would have written a letter to the people who made those trolleys and said what a good precision job they made of the bearings and the axles.

But they wouldn't appreciate my letter; I didn't have any bit of paper saying I was an engineer, so I couldn't have an opinion. The trolley stopped when it fell over in the gutter, the plates went furthest. Lucky there was no one crossing the corridors in its way; it didn't even hit a car or

147

anything, but a blue metal truck roared up and tried to get by the plates. You should have seen it, the driver tried to pick his way through it very slow out of respect for the hospital, but he didn't actually want to get down and pick them up. I don't blame him. The plates crunched slow and very loud.

One of them snapped with a sound very like the tuning fork the teacher had when I was in fifth class. I don't mean the sort of sound, I mean the same note. You'd never believe it, but I was a soprano once. Old Mr Hocking or Pryce with a y would disown me now, but they thought a lot of me then and my voice like a bell, as Hocking said.

When I got back inside I got my collar sort of neat and parted my hair and the nurses ate out of my hand. If I'd come back in the room untidy they would have hated me and they'd probably have accused me of the trolley bit. It's amazing how easy you can lead people on by your appearance.

I passed the exact door I tore my leather coat on one night when I'd visited my brother. It was a Yale lock with the latch out and I was in a hurry to get home. I suppose I was always in a hurry to get visits over. I wonder if he ever knew before he died how I hated visiting him? I never even contradicted the house doctor that Monday morning when he told me and my other brother that it was no use giving him another transfusion. Without actually saying it he made us think the poor kid would never leave the bed anyway, never be able to get on his feet again. So we didn't stick up for a few more weeks of life for him. We just let him die like a dog, like the doctor wanted. I suppose they wanted the bed. They'd been pretty good to him, letting him go home weekends and the bed still there for him on Monday mornings. When he waved goodbye and I was at the door his face was so white it reminded me of when he was a kid. When he was a baby he lay on his back for thirty months and he was white as the sheets around him. But no one ever wondered if there was something wrong. He bled for a week when he got a tooth out, so some wisdom in Ma got her to teach him to look after his teeth so he wouldn't have any more out.

I settled in my bed. I was pretty tired, my eyes drooped. A kooka was on the verandah sill, his cocked head very still. I sat up in bed watching him, then when he pushed up into the air and flew away his windy wing flap startled me.

What with all that exertion I started on my old trick of getting sore eyes; I'm sure they were full of gravel and sand, they were so dry and irritated. I fell back on the pillow and shut my eyes and imagined I was in the bush looking down on a cold jutting rock, there was a great singer standing on it, don't ask me how he got out here to this dead hole of a country, so I made him sing a very sentimental song that I'd heard come from an opera called the 'Girlfishes'. I still seem to hear it now, and anytime I want my eyes irrigated I imagine that song, and it works. I'm very sentimental really. I can listen to a sad thing or something sentimental about someone's kid, and the tears bubble up in my eyes. I can even imagine I'm listening to someone, in fact it's better that way; with someone around, I have to think continually if they're about to clobber me, or something. After all, I'd do the same if someone was silly enough to shut his eyes with me around.

The bed got more and more comfortable, my eyes didn't sting any more and my head travelled back to Bee. Last time I was at the house she was on about the weather. Usually nothing ever worried her, but she carried on about what the scientists were not doing about the weather.

'If they want different weather for Sydney, or any other place, why don't they make it by putting up mountains and making more lakes. They can do it with their silly big bombs. They could make weather traps.'

I couldn't talk for a little while. Bee didn't usually say more than a few words, she was wound up that time. I asked her why she got so het up about weather, but she must have thought she'd said enough. She wouldn't say any more, only that she'd been reading some books. It made me wonder, that sudden belt of talking, if the weather was what she was really worried about. Maybe she was worried about the kids. Or me.

What did Ma and my old man think they were doing? Did they get together some cold night when they were too tired and miserable to do anything else? Was it a last resort, before they cut their throats? Were they desperate? I'm glad I don't know. I don't really want to find out I'm the product of something so casual that I nearly didn't happen.

Poor Ma. When she couldn't get us to do what she wanted by asking, she thought she could hurt us by hurting herself. She never woke up that it was impossible. No one who looked at us and heard us talk would ever think we'd suffer to see anyone in pain. Even a mother.

The verandah creaked with the sun leaving it, just like it creaked mornings with the sun getting under its skin. The plastic sheeting under me, in case I wet the bed, creaked too.

Pretty soon nothing creaked. I was far gone in a dream. I was surrounded by this tree, full of prickles, this prickly tree had its arms round me so I couldn't get out. I couldn't call out for help because there was a great thorn under my chin and others on all sides of my head, in fact the more I looked round to explore the dream, the more thorns I found lined up on me. Some people came round the tree and I tried to signal them to get me out, but no matter how I moved I came up against these needle thorns. I couldn't speak, couldn't move, all I could do was move my eyes from side to side. That saved me. There was one man looking right into the tree, right at me, but it was dark and all he could see was a darkness. I was moving my eyes from side to side, trying to let the light flash on them, when I saw what they had in their hands. They were out to get me. Some had shotguns, some had mattock handles, some had axes, some knives, some just rocks. And now I looked closely they were all in uniforms. What had I done? I must have done something pretty terrible this time, but I couldn't think what it was. I was stiff with fright, and woke up soaked. Sweat ran down the back of my head. The top of my back near the neck was all water, I was water everywhere.

I guess you could say I went to water. Nurses were round the bed when I woke, and there was a screen. I couldn't even see any of the nasty patients, or the dying

151

ones. I quieted down right away so they wouldn't give me any needles to put me off. After dark they went away and took the screen. I was shaking and had pains all over me, but I went out. I knew I was the same person, with the same strength, no matter what condition I was in; all I had to do was prove it to myself.

What if that thing was happening to me now? The thing I always felt was just round the corner for me. Perhaps it was a sickness. I tried my strength on a fence, one of those wooden fences white with enamel paint. I had to dig my heels in at the edge of the concrete footpath and push with everything I had against that fence. It worked. I broke the fence and woke the people's dog, but I walked on pretty happy, because it showed I hadn't lost one bit of strength; I was only sweating because I was sick besides. I hate the sound of dogs barking, so I trotted on down the street to Edgeworth David Avenue and I was so happy I still had my muscles that I lifted the front end of a small car parked outside the corner shop so that the back was up to a street tree and the front nestled in behind a lamp-post. Whoever owned that would have to get help, unless he was strong as me. I had to breathe extra hard, though, but that's not hard to understand when you remember I was sick.

I walked back to the hospital, I didn't want to go home and give Bee or the kids whatever germs I had. The shivers got me before I got to my ward, it was hard walking, so I forced myself to trot again. That always made me feel better. Unfortunately I trotted into a wall just where I thought there was a long empty room. They carried me back inside.

That was nice of them. I asked them to carry me very carefully, so they wouldn't break the bubbles. I was carrying a trayful of bubbles. The tray was about a foot wide and the bubbles were about two inches round, but the bubbles kept expanding, I had to keep my hands on them to try to stop them getting too big and beyond me. I tried to contain them. It was hopeless. They got bigger and bigger, they slipped through my fingers, they forced my hands wide apart, they were going to expand to the size of separate worlds. The tray was yards wide and I was way above them and much bigger, myself, to try to master them, but it was no use. No matter what way my dream twisted and turned and grew and tried to cope with the expanding bubbles, which were now like great balloons big enough to carry a man into the air, no matter what I did, the bubbles forced me back.

I came awake fighting for breath, although at the back of my mind I knew I wasn't really suffocating.

'Open the doors!' I howled.

'Open the doors and I can breathe!' I kept on like that very loud for a long time until they had to call the house doctor and he tried to talk me out of it—he didn't want anything like this getting to the ears of the local Board—but in the end all the doors in the hospital were opened. They tricked me, partly, because I know for sure that one door was closed without them telling me, but I must have been too tired to insist; I let them kid me. I went to sleep peacefully. It was great being able to breathe.

Maybe I'm only alive when I'm dreaming. I don't know. But I could see our old goat plain as day in my dream, butting the little old fibro toilet down the yard, and I could hear Ma inside yelling help! I ambled down to pull the goat away and tie him up a bit further on where he could nibble the blackies in peace and on the way down the steps a terrific wind blew up and knocked next door's toilet flat with only the pan standing. Black and shiny and squat. I know those things happened weeks apart but, dreaming, they both got in together.

Sure enough when I rescued Ma, it wasn't Ma. It was Bee. So we went out all dressed up—no car so I had to take the train—and they held us up at the ticket office. Some old woman trying to get a ticket for his cat. He was tweedy and old and so was the cat. He should have shoved it in a shoe box with a few holes for air. I started to tell him this, but the words changed into asking Bee why she didn't hang around more at home with her legs up like the girls in the magazines, but she took no notice and helped me onto the train, telling me to mind my step for I was now a small kid in white socks and short pants. We got to the ceremony in Sydney, they'd cleared the traffic off the Bridge and all the important people were there sweating in their dark clothes and all the workers were there and all the kids were there but they had light summer things and were quite comfortable.

It turned out there was a war starting and they had the ministers and priests blessing the flag, then blessing the soldiers' bayonets and rifles—it took an awful long time— saying prayers and more blessings for the jet fighters and the navy ships and all their vehicles and all the servicemen and everything. At last they wheeled up a huge big bomb and blessed that, only they called it a device. Nuclear device.

154

However the bomb was too much and the Bridge broke and everything sank except the children, who swam to shore. Luckily Bee was a small kid now, like me, and when we got to shore all we could see of the ceremony was a small piece of paper floating around in the harbour breeze. I knew without catching it, that it had the bomb formula written on, you know, the E equals MC squared bit we learned at school. Unfortunately one of the kids, his daddy must have been a general, rescued it and tried to drum up a bit of a procession with it, holding it up as if he'd found the holy grail. It was only paper, after all.

Then somehow we were in the sportsground with millions of other kids. One of the kids whose daddy was a minister before he sank, had taken over from his old man and organised a religious service. Talk out your troubles, he boomed over the PA system. So the kids all obeyed and talked out their troubles to each other, except no one listened, so they were talking to themselves—the row was tremendous. Sit and think, boomed over the mike, so everyone sat and thought. The leader'd had enough. But while it was quiet with only the noise of millions of kids breathing, the general's son grabbed the mike off the other kid and yelled: Make the army your Korea! There were too many leaders for me. The big people sinking hadn't changed a thing. Soon some bosses' sons would get kids to follow them, other kids would take refuge in the army, everyone would be looking for someone to lean on, no one wanted to be his own boss.

I turned to go. I was about to ask Bee if she wanted to go, but she was only another sort of thing for me to lean on, so I was glad when I looked down and found she'd turned into a magazine and I was carrying her under my arm. But magazines were only another sort of thing to hide in, so I gave her to some little kids who looked lost.

The sound of a mower woke me, the sort a man sits on, and I woke up thinking of my old man and how his constant companions in his last years were the Bible and Yates Garden Guide. Don't ask me why that got into my head after my crazy dream.

So there I was. Clapped out at sixteen and three-quarters. They set a wardsman in a brown uniform to watch me, and I was so weak in their rotten bed that I didn't even object. For the first few days. Then it got to me that here was a uniform that had caught up with me and I started to worry. What if this joker had something to do with the others that had been following me?

I had to get out of there. When he went out for something I started to leave, but I was so weak on my pins I decided I'd better go back and put up with it until I was better.

The worst break I had in years, when I got back to the ward they strapped me down, rolled me onto a trolley, raced me down a corridor and down a ramp and whipped out my tonsils, just to teach me a lesson, and when I was back in bed the next day a kid I hadn't seen for years or at least months visited me and gave me a swig out of his bottle of gin.

13
SCHOOL OF ARTS

Sometimes everything in my chest swirls. I think I must have got away from that hospital too soon. They all had smiles on their faces, thinking of the lesson their surgeon taught me about not getting into the hands of anyone with some authority that you get from a piece of paper. I wonder if they had anything more to smile about? They didn't tell me what they found out about me.

The best thing seems to be to take pretty deep breaths, not too quick, then relax and breathe out; if I force the breath out I get the thump in the chest. This way it's only a tumbling in the chest, like the waves that hit the rocks then tumble and swirl about in the crevices and gaps as the sea sucks them out again for another attack. I was hiding up in a sort of loft inside the School of Arts, amongst the kids' medicine balls and caretaker's ladders and old advertising boards. You get to it by going in the room just inside the front door, the room with the sink and cupboards and the manhole in the ceiling. When you get up there you take the step-ladder with you, and also, if you don't like dust, you take up a wet rag and wipe over everything. The loft thing projects into the main hall and has a wood decoration in front of it, so you can't be seen from the stage, neither can the mess of wood and cardboard things.

If you're hearing a steady stream of noise and something gets between you and the noise, you'll notice the interruption. The gutter water in the street after the rain was dribbling its little quick song and I heard it suddenly cut in two. It hit me with a hard blow, I was liking the sound of that gutter water. A leg with a lot of bone in it hit the metal of a car, the venetians on the front windows of the School of Arts clattered as the door opened. An old man's neck clicked. It was a society meeting, I had to lie low for a couple of hours, trying not to laugh at the things they said. They wouldn't have liked the thought of a stranger listening to their minutes and their points of order and their votes and notices of motion.

They wouldn't like me at all, and what that sort of people don't like is bad. Very bad. Delinquent. They're the ones that are always saying how bad the juvenile menace is growing. But nowadays there's more juveniles, so naturally our output is up, but you can see from what I've told you that there are a lot of kids that don't do much harm at all. I do enough for a couple of dozen.

The kids that belonged to the Church Youth had a lot of fun with their games of kiss in the ring and postman's knock. Until I saw them at it I had no idea there were still such old games going on. From where I was up there I was the only one who could see what they got up to when their head man, about forty, was out.

I tried to teach myself to play the piano at night after the last of the meetings had finished, and after a few days I could get a tune out of it, but it sounded so thin just playing the one note at a time that I couldn't stand it any longer. I just couldn't get the idea of thinking about the bottom notes at the same time as the main tune.

One man worried me. That was the man who had a notebook and a pen and counted the people at most of the meetings. It seemed to me I had seen his kind before; not that he was in a uniform, unless you count a dark suit, white shirt, and tie as a uniform. He got on my works so much that I got down from my perch one afternoon when there was a church fraternisation meeting and walked out in front of the lot of them as soon as he went round the back of the hall to the toilets. One look at my leather coat and they all saw I came from a bent and badly broken home where no one went to church. There was a feeling in the air as if all I needed was to go back to church with them and all would be well.

I was halfway out when I felt the feeling of the meeting change. All of a sudden I had become the ringleader of the gang of kids that enticed the innocent young High School girls down into the backyard of the hall of an afternoon and forced them to sell their bodies to the High School boys for the modest sum of a few shillings or a packet of potato chips or the promise to take them to a dance on Saturday

159

night. I was the cause of the pregnancy rate in second and third-year girls being at an all-time high. I was so sure of the way they felt that I said to them all, 'Calm down, people. There's schools out past Parramatta that leave these High Schools for dead. There was a hundred and three pregnant girls last year at one near Blacktown.'

I was out the door while they still had their mouths open. I didn't tell them about the little girls that paid the boys two or three bob just to find out what it was like. Perhaps they weren't thinking that at all. I mean, about me being the cause of schoolgirls' moral downfall.

Maybe I had made a mistake and the feeling in the air was just like the one that used to be around at home when I had taken my sick brother's friends. I didn't use the ladder getting down; I would have to move a table over under the manhole if I was going in there again.

What a fluke! That my parents had me. They could easily have had a girl. Maybe they'd have lived longer.

I wish I knew who's got Ma's photos. They should have left me a share, I don't even have one with the old man when he was a kid in the war, or Ma when she was a girl. I know they all thought I got the good ones, but I was the only one that didn't rat them out of the old photo box.

I went home. I wish I could have cabbed it. But. No dough, I had to leg it. It was a relief to hear the voices of the kids.

'What kind of day did you have at school?' I asked Stevo. That was the sort of question Bee usually asked him.

'Oh, fairly splendid and a bit ordinary,' came the answer.

'Any composition today?' I asked him.

'He wrote you a poem today,' Bee answered. She fished a paper out of the kitchen drawer. It said,

> To Daddy—a poem. Shoes.
> Shoes, shoes, shoes, who wants shoes,
> Shoes at Grace Brothers, shoes at Woolworths,
> Shoes in windows like tree leaves pointing at you,
> Shoes, shoes, who wants shoes.

I was about to say what a good poem it was, but he had a whip.

'Look at this whip,' he ordered me. It was a whip of plastic-sheathed wire and a deal handle. 'It's fast and fascinating.' He slashed it about. I whipped out of the way; if I hadn't, I'd have lost skin. You've got to have skin.

'Pass the soap, Stevo,' Bee asked. We were in the kitchen. He passed the soap.

'No more asking for things.' Doing what he was told was a considerable strain. I liked that.

'Brush your hair, sonny boy,' commanded Bee. And gave him the hard brush. It used to make the kids' faces and heads shine. He brushed.

'It looks marvellous at the back. It looks marvellous at the front, too.' She hadn't bothered to teach him to be nasty to himself and always say his own things were crook.

'Do your hair as soon as Stevo's finished,' Bee said to Chris.

'Can't. I'm busy crying.' She was. She blubbered a lot.

'You can have fresh water in your bath,' promised Bee.

'Can I wash my hair?' pleaded Chris.

'All right. It won't hurt her,' Bee explained.

'Wash my hair in cool fresh water, then,' demanded Chris. If you gave her one little favour, she bargained for half a dozen more. While Bee was getting Allie ready for bed, Stevo and Chris made a pretending house to live in, right down to a television set.

'Get out of my way,' I heard Chris say. 'That's the TV. Get out of my way, I can't see the TV.' I suppose Bee must have done all the work she did mainly to be there when they came out with things like that.

'What did you learn at Scripture today, Chris?' asked Bee. Must have been Wednesday. I don't usually keep track of the days, one is just like another to me.

'Kiddies that have things and bring them out in the playground should share them if they're lollies,' answered Chris.

'Where does that minister at Scripture get all his ideas from?' demanded Stevo, then went straight on to ask me to put my finger in his fist. He made a fist with a hole in it, and the hole pointing up.

'Now put your finger in.' I did that.

'Now stir it round.' I did.

'Now you're cleaning the toilet!'

'Where did you get that sort of joke from, Stephen?' asked Bee, looking severe. But she spoiled the effect by being in the middle of getting them some biscuits with butter and jam on. Stevo took advantage of that. You can't say he wasn't quick on the uptake.

'Can I help you, Mum? You can butter it and I'll jam it.'

162

Naturally she forgot her question, but Stevo was so used to winning that sort of skirmish, he didn't even look triumphant.

'How about some Chantic Bird tonight?' I asked. I wanted to stay on the good side of Bee and also I was starting to get pretty curious about the bird. He didn't hear.

'What about that frantic bird, man?' He managed a bit of a smile. I'll say this for him, he didn't always pretend my weak old jokes were funny. I kidded him along a little and pretty soon he got onto the story. I was hoping he would start it and go right through—I liked hearing it over again. But no. All he would do was take up where he left off.

The bird was a captive. Someone must have been jealous, though, because the King received in the post a box with a clockwork bird in it, a bird covered with diamonds, sapphires, rubies. Only one of the real bird's tunes in it, but everyone liked looking at the sparkling jewels rather than the grey feathers of the real bird. The new bird with one song was something they could be proud of.

The real bird flew away to her green trees by the sea and the fishermen were glad and the common people, but the King banished her because she took her freedom. Without even waiting in her cage to beg for it.

One day, after a thousand performances, the clock-work bird cracked a spring and all the wheels gnashed against each other. They repaired it well enough to have it sing once a year.

Then the King caught asiatic flu or something and was dying. Death sat on his chest, and his bad and good deeds were peering at him round corners.

163

But the Chantic Bird had heard and came to the palace and sat on a branch outside the King's window and sang all her sweetest songs, like bells of glass tinkling in the evening of the world. The Bird enticed Death away and earned the only reward she wanted, a tear from the King's eye. This time she demanded freedom to fly about outside and to come and sing when she wanted to. The King said yes, since his bargaining power was nil.

Stevo lost interest after this and I didn't feel like begging anyone to carry on with something they didn't want to do.

I went for a walk, it was still light, and as I walked I thought what a queer individual I must have seemed, playing football down on Pennant Hills oval and dreaming half the time. If the day was nice and I didn't really feel like it, I'd look over the tops of the trees surrounding the ground, and let my head fly away in dreams. Miles away. The people in the stand and barracking on the hill must have wondered who was the one with concussion.

When I look back at the pages done, I surprise myself that all those words were in the typewriter keys.

My folks carried me round in a suitcase when I was a baby. They had no baby pram. There was even a photo of me and the case. I wonder who got that one, too?

It was such a clear afternoon and seeing the workers come home from captivity made me feel so good that I decided Bee should have something to celebrate with. I got into a certain church nearby—there were seven in half a mile—and helped them get rid of a dozen bottles of altar wine. And while I was there I took a Bible for Ma, and it wasn't until I was outside that I remembered she was dead. I kept it, anyway.

I had a bad feeling about the way Ma died. Of all the family that died, I visited her the least. The others went in shifts, to cover the times when she'd be without visitors, but not me. No one was actually game to tell me I ought to go, but I could feel the way they thought. I was there when her old ticker stopped, but she didn't know. I was doing a pretty complicated sum about interest on a quarterly reducing balance at four and a half per cent the day she was in the coma, and I had hold of her hand when she took the last few breaths. For some reason, the others didn't want to see the last of her.

As I remember it, there were thirteen steps up our old back verandah and Ma had to climb them a million times a day. No, there were fourteen steps. You had to count the one at the top to make it fourteen, but that still is fourteen.

Sometimes I can go into a sort of trance and bring back people I knew once. I was thinking of the fourteen steps and how they made no difference at all to my old man; sick or well he didn't let steps beat him; I was thinking very hard, forcing my head muscles in the hope that they'd bring fresh thoughts along with fresh blood to my brain, when it started to work. My eyes were tight, my face straining in concentration and the face of my old man gradually appeared in a sort of whitish mist, giving it the look of glowing. There was a rushing sound, as if he had come on a high wind.

I couldn't call it a coloured dream, there was only the face by itself. The rest was darkness.

Without thinking about it, I had strolled back to the School of Arts and I rubbered into the first room, without noticing how easy it had been to get in. The door was open, and I heard the sound of a hat being pushed back on a man's head. I cornered towards him and there was a man inside the main hall, with a pad and pencil in his hands, making notes. He was pretending to count the chairs, but I knew right enough that he was probably on my track. I got out of there.

When I left the School of Arts I felt sort of hungry.

14

OFFICE BLOCK

Sheilas with great thick kneebones had been sitting at those office desks all day, and there I was after everyone had left, making drawings under the boss's desk. It was like being in a forest of parking meters, in a way, or in a drive-in when no one else was there; there was space for people and you knew people were there every day, but without the people the desks and the chairs were just waiting, helpless. It wasn't time for the cleaners yet, I had to go upstairs and really hide when the cleaners got there.

I was looking upside down at the underside of this big desk, wondering how many years it would be before my little message got through to some office explorer, when I got itchy on the left side of that big bone that sticks out at the back of your neck where your neck joins on to your back. At the same time as I scratched it with my fingernail,

I got a tingling feeling on the left hand side of my face halfway between the ear and the jaw and a bit underneath. When I stopped scratching, it stopped tingling. When I did it again, it tingled; very piercing it was. I started to wonder if there were a few wires crossed somewhere, there must have been a hook-up between two sets of nerves; maybe the one nerve was doing two jobs. I tell you, it got me in. But only for a while. You can go queer if you let yourself think about little things like that for too long.

Did you know you can have the use of a toilet in the city any time you like? All you have to do is walk in, no one asks who you are, no one owns the places, no one cares what happens to them, no one is game to ask anyone else questions in case he gets a kick in die face or a savage reply. But some of them are locked. Bosses have to have privileges, not waiting for others to finish, and not to have to use the seat that others have sat on with their dirty bottoms. You can be sure that not everyone has sat on those toilets; no worker is going to ask the boss for that key. If you want to use those locked ones, climb over like I did, and if the owner comes along and rattles the door trying to get in, all you have to do is make a terrific noise, with shouting and singing out and all that; people in the city hate noise in the toilet. They get embarrassed, which is funny; they always reckon they're so sexy and loose, but in my opinion country people have it all over city people as far as sex goes. And all sorts of natural behaviour.

There was a carpet in the office I had, and it was good to lie down on; you couldn't feel the cold of the concrete underneath. It gave me warnings, too; the sound of feet scrooching on hard office carpet, when you've got your ear to it, is a give-away for anyone coming.

Across George Street, in the doorways of the old Millard's building, there was a man and a woman, in broad daylight, doing their best to get together. They were only tormenting each other; if they'd been out in the country they could have hopped in the car and driven out on the highway a bit and ducked into the scrub and laid down like beachtowels, together. I couldn't see that they'd do any good in a doorway.

As a sort of accompaniment, or sound cover, an old Broomwade compressor was doing about fifteen hundred revs, from the sound of it, twenty yards from a team of workers with jackhammers, making another hole in the streets of Sydney. The lovers were getting on with the matter in hand, people were looking at the noise more than at them, and I thought I'd give them a hand; I went down to a newsagent in Castlereagh and got some bangers, went back and threw them down in George Street. That scattered the street-people and the two in the doorway did more and more to each other, until I couldn't stand it any longer and kept away from the window. What I did wasn't as bad as when I got up the top of the Mutual Insurance Building—that's a place that's wide open; you can go up the top any time and climb onto the top of the lift well—that was when I threw pies down into Hosking, or over the wall into Martin Place.

I had a rest on the carpet in the office and spent a bit of time remembering the happy times I'd had, like in a newsreel one day and a huge fat ex-Labor politician sitting with his daughter behind me, talking loud so that no one could hear what was going on. I turned round and said 'Shut up!' That was the only time I've ever spoken to a politician, or one has spoken to me. He started to say I shouldn't interrupt what an important man has to say because the most casual thing he said was worth a whole lifetime of what I said—he didn't exactly say all that, but I knew he was going to from the way he looked.

So I said, 'Shovatt!' and he shut up; they don't like their names being mentioned when there's criticism going on.

I got up to go and get something to read. Dymock's wasn't far away; boy, we used to give them a caning when I was at High School, hardly a week passed when we didn't have dictionaries or notebooks to sell to the kids that didn't go through the city on the way home. All I could get, though, was a tiny book in an orange cover. It turned out to be a Russian grammar. I hardly had the thing in my kick, standing near a corner of the shelves upstairs, when a hand seemed to come from round the bend and touched me on the trouser. You might think it was an accident and the hand was looking for books, but believe me, I had no books where that hand touched me. I don't like that sort of thing, there were enough kids like that at school, but at least they had the decency to come right out and ask you, or if they were shy of talking they'd do something for you, a favour, and keep doing things for you until you sort of grinned at them and then you'd be talking together and pretty soon you'd find yourself walking home with them and no one else around and when they wanted you to look at something they'd grab your hand. Don't get me wrong, I'm not one

170

of those phonies that sees something clammy and weak in all the poor devils that want you to like them—want boys to like them—but it gets a bit too much when they try to sneak a kiss, or watch you and look right in your eyes and pay attention to what you say as if you were important. It makes you very uneasy.

But this hand round a corner, I didn't like it. So what I did, it was pretty mean, but men like that take a risk all the time, they know they have to get caught a fair percentage of the time; what I did was whip out the book and put it in the hand then make a terrific noise so that the counter-jumpers across the way looked up and saw this hand with the book in it. He had to pay for it. The floorwalker or whatever he was lugged him down to the manager's office and a few of the shoppers noticed what was going on; that was good enough, usually they wouldn't know if you were up beside them. If I hadn't made such a noise they would have given me a reward, I think; but they were a bit suspicious of why I made such a fuss. The floorwalker said thank you very much, but he was the sort that wouldn't give you the smell of an oilrag, I could see that.

The poofter was dragged off, down the stairs to the main floor, and as he went he called out, 'I love you, Michael. I still love you.' What a thing to say. I didn't want to stick around and explain that my name wasn't Michael, so I got another thin book in my shirt and out.

Back to the office. I settled down again on the carpet to read the book. It turned out to be pacifist poetry, of all things, and I'll tell you it was certainly a weak character that wrote that book; I bet he couldn't stand the sight of his own blood, let alone someone else's. Me, I think wars have to be. While two people in this world argue and don't see eye to eye, there'll be wars. It's no great distance between an argument with words and one with fists and one with guns, but a lot of people think there's a big difference. Which shows how wrong they can be if they've never heard of temperaments like mine. And like yours, Stevo, I hope.

It wasn't much comfort to me, but I had to do something. I lifted the tops of the metal filing cabinets—it doesn't take much muscle—and pulled the drawers out. That way you don't need a key. Then I changed papers from file to file, there must have been thousands of bits of paper in those drawers, all standing on edge in light brown folders, I made such a thorough job of it that I bet they had to burn the papers rather than take the trouble to fit them together again. If they decided to get them in order, though, there'd be employment for a worker; that's a main consideration, they tell me. Why they kept the papers, though that's the real mystery. Sometimes I've heard office people talk and I've thought I've been on the track of what they see in all their papers. The ones I heard talking spoke as if the papers themselves, or the words written on them, had a life of their own. They even sounded to me as if the life the papers had, or the words, was a different kind of life, even a better sort of life than what us ordinary people have. And that's just silly. It's almost as if the papers and the words are a higher race of being that have to be protected; the men I heard talking started to come more alive when they got down to looking at them and reading the words. Perhaps their minds were on the papers, not in their bodies, and

172

they only really lived when they dug out the paper words. I don't know.

I suppose by now you've guessed that that sort of thing is beyond me; I'm no good at working out other people. You need a different sort of brain for that. More sympathetic.

Thinking gets you into trouble. I'd been so far away in my head that I didn't hear the cleaner coming. The first I knew was an interruption to the sound coming into my head; there was something between me and the steady stream of sound. I was so startled that I jumped up and clobbered the cleaner just as he came in the door; I felt a bit bad because he had gear in both hands, it wasn't quite a fair thing. Besides, I outweighed him. That always gets me. Right here.

He made a sound like when the dressing had to be changed on Stevo's leg. Remember? The leg I scalded. And down he went, his face looking like old Mr Kelly when he came to where I worked one day and asked me for his shotgun back that I took. The stinking people next door rang up and told him they saw me climb in the window.

With him breathing heavy on the floor and me feeling miserable, the windows started to look like cemetery slabs, the desks like graveyard memorials. When I stood up, the desks looked like a forest of memorials to the dead.

As I climbed over the grille into the top floor of the Arcade, I wondered to myself was it the old man's or was it Ma's egg that was sour?

The trees round St Andrew's were shaken in the wind, their sound reached down to me walking in George Street. As a

173

matter of fact, their sound was a bit like long arms sweeping out from the trunks of the trees, flailing.

I walked round a bit, but couldn't make up my mind where to go. What I did, I went back and down under the Town Hall steps, you know the little underpass where the Mayor's Rolls pulls up. At night it's nice and dark and no one bothers you if you stay out of sight. As nights go, it wasn't a bad one, the concrete wasn't too cold on my back and I got involved in this red and white dream. I was in an old town—I'll think of the name in a minute—and I was higher than all the buildings and the light poles and every building was red and white. Even the spires on the old convict churches were shorter than me; I could reach down and have them tickle my hand, no trouble at all. The people in the streets—I didn't remember them in my dream but I can see them now—were like ants. You know ants, they fool a lot of people, but have you ever watched them? If you do, it'll open your eyes. They run around like mad; the hotter the day the faster they run, but they get nowhere. I never know who they're trying to fool, but they fool someone; they really get their tucker under false pretences. Well, the citizens of Puddingate Bridge were like that. That was the name of the town. In the dream.

But the thing about the dream was that I was frightened. I was at the mercy of the red and white. The glare of it hit me. Somehow having actual bright red and real white both having a go at me made me very on edge. Why would anyone be scared because of a couple of colours? I suppose it has happened before, specially if the colours were the colours of enemy flags or uniforms or the wing-dots on bombers.

174

I woke up leaving a stain on the concrete where I touched it. A sweat stain. It was only another place I had to get out of. There were a good many people on the streets, so since I needed a few dollars I got up and walked to Woolworths' corner and started a bit of a song. Singing made me feel better. Don't get me wrong; I can't sing for nuts. But making a noise was a good antidote for the feeling I had about the red and white dream. I got enough money for a few beers and after I swallowed them I sang louder and got more.

I had a lot of fun walking along in the street talking to people.

You had to have a doorway handy or a corner to duck round, not because they'd chase you, but they turn round and stare after you and if they see you talk to someone else they stop worrying and trying to remember who you are, but if you just duck off out of sight they're still fretting.

'How's the goldfish, Gerald?' That's the one I started with.

'What's good for acne?' An old lady about forty started to give me a few remedies, but young girls were the best ones to ask.

'Did you get your membership card yet?' That was a good one for men over twenty, that's about the age they start worrying about what they belong to.

'Why did they turf you out?' That was for men, too. They're always easy marks for the worry wart.

'Turn it a fraction to the right. Just a fraction.' That was for anyone that looked like a car driver, but any nut drives a car.

'Has she had the baby yet?' That made them go red. People don't like to be the centre of attention, they expect to get out boldly in public, but stay private.

Was there rust inside it, as well?' People are ashamed of rust.

I stayed there till I got sick of city faces, then I hopped a train and back to the sticks where I belonged. Actually it wasn't very distant sticks, but far enough away to make me feel different. And better. I had a brush with a snapper on the train and I had to back up right to the last carriage, where I let him corner me right at the back of the train. I didn't feel much like smacking him over the skull, so I pretended to go through all my pockets and some I didn't have until we reached a station. It was only about five miles I had to go, so I waited until the train was moving out of the platform, pushed past him and off the train and started walking. I felt a bit of a coward, getting away sort of sneaky and not over his dead body, so to speak.

Suddenly it was a cold night and I couldn't help thinking of my brother's plaque stuck on a crematorium wall—Northern Suburbs—on a niche which may or may not have contained his ashes, out in the wind and the cold. Just stuck there. When you visit, it's a nuisance if you strike a day when a lot died and they shoved them in the same wall. You can't move for mourners, and people start swearing and treading on kids. And there's no place to stick a flower. And maybe not even any ashes in the hole. A lot of people have nightmares about that, not only me. How does anyone really know they burn the bodies? If a few ashes is all they have to show for a corpse, they could ship the bodies out at night to medical schools and burn grass clippings instead. No one would know...It's the first thing I would think of.

There it goes again. I'm noticing that a lot lately. I no sooner finish talking about something else than I'm back on to myself again. Sometimes I make me sick. Getting soft.

I sneaked in the house and slept the rest of the night out up in the ceiling, and when small bits of the morning poked through the old nail holes in the iron roof I was awake and listening to the kids making their talk about the world, what they could see of it.

Stevo was sitting up in bed by then, reading. Nothing could break his concentration. After Bee had tried to get an answer out of him for a while she got a bit sharp. I suppose you couldn't blame her, and tiptoed into the room and gave him a Boo! just behind him, but it hardly shook him more than a foot upwards. She had to laugh, and asked him how he felt.

'I'm feeling not pretty well and the only thing I can do is pray.' You could see all the sharpness had gone out of Bee.

'What you reading, Stevo?'

'A book.'

'Are they nice people in it?' He looked at her.

'Why do all my friends get killed?'

'What friends?'

'Even in books.'

'I guess the people that make the books consider your friends have had their turn to live and now it's their turn to die.'

'Does everyone die, Mum?'

'Everyone that has a turn to live, has a turn to die.'

'Even you, Mum?'

'Of course.'

'Me too?'

'You've got a fine long time to go, sonny boy. There's a lot of years to be happy about yet.'

'Mum, can we leave the front door open all day today?'

'The front door's open most days. I'll make sure we keep it open today, son.' You could see he wanted her to ask why.

'Are you expecting a visitor, Stevo?'

'Oh, someone might drop in to explain something.'

'Could I explain it?'

'No, it's not in my head yet. It isn't anything for you to worry about, Mum. But it makes me lonely when everyone has to have their turn to die.'

Bee didn't say anything to that.

'It'll be your turn first, Mum, won't it?'

'Yes, son. You won't have to worry for a long time.'

'What will Chris and me and Allie do then?'

'You'll be fine big people then. Everything will be different.'

'Won't we care?'

'I suppose you will, but you won't cry. I think we've talked enough about that, Stevo.' Stevo wasn't going to admit anything, but fortunately at that moment Chris ran and fell over the little step into the lounge room where the floorboards had a bump in them. She cried, and ran to Bee's lap.

'I know how to make you better—ice-cream.' She patted Chris's hair.

'I know how to make you better, Christine,' corrected Stevo. 'Jesus and God will make you better. They're good and kind.' I bet the scripture teacher would have been surprised to know that anyone ever remembered what she taught the kids on Wednesdays.

These things didn't fix Chris, though, so Bee got the breakfast ready. When Chris felt she hadn't been kidded to enough and balked at eating Bee's hash because it had spinach in it, Stevo came to the rescue again.

'Popeye gets spinach in his tummy. He gets it from the big girl that's always in trouble.' That fixed Chris. Out the kitchen window the kids could see who was passing in the street. I could hear the steps of a heavy man on the bitumen.

'What was that on the man?'

'Don't know,' said Bee. 'Wasn't looking.'

'You'll have to watch it, Mum,' said Chris severely.

'It was a sugar bag on his shoulder for carrying wood from the bush,' said Stevo. He was usually positive.

'Any weddings today, Mum?' asked Chris. It was Saturday and Bee had taken them to a wedding of one of her brothers a couple of Saturdays ago.

'I don't like weddings,' said Stevo. 'I don't want to put heavy wedding things on.' He had had to put on a white frilly shirt and blue satin trousers. I was lousy enough to call him Esmeralda and it stuck in his head. 'I just want to go to see people.'

They were starting to split up, as a group I mean; Bee couldn't keep them still for very long just talking to them. Chris pinched Stevo's mouth organ, Stevo whacked

Chris, Bee whacked Stevo, Stevo cried, Chris blew the mouth organ.

'I can't love you any more,' cried Stevo. 'I'm in jail and the doors are locked.' Poor little kid. Even Allie was sorry for him, she big-eyed him and went on slobbering, dripping with tucker.

'Mum,' asked Chris, holding up the wet mouth organ, 'Why is the music always there? Why doesn't it wear out?'

That gave Stevo his chance, tears and all.

'The music isn't there all the time. It's not there till you blow it.' That was a triumph, knowing something.

Chris said, 'You're healthy. You're brave, aren't you? Why should you cry about everything?' I think she was a bit tougher than Stevo. I remember the other day he pulled her leg and she fell off the lowboy, but she didn't put him in. Not many little kids are as independent as that, specially girls. Girls are great dobbers.

'Can I play over in Janet's before she comes home from school?' said Chris. She loved clambering over the big rocks.

'Not while she's out,' Bee commanded.

'Is it against the law of other people's property?'

Somehow I didn't like getting down from the ceiling while they were there, I waited until Bee started on the washing and the kids went out playing. Stevo wouldn't want to be telling me his bird story, not when he could be playing. I went round to the old cricket pitch where we used to play when we were kids, it was shady there. I thought how different the world was now from then, when all we had to do was trot round and play when we wanted to. I still did, but there was no one else wanted to. I bowled a few rocks along the wicket, it was concrete and the rocks skidded nicely under the bats of the invisible batsmen. I got out about as many batsmen as the rocks I bowled.

People want you to be a tidy number doing a tidy job and no questions asked and no complaints. And people want to do that themselves, as if being born was a mistake and they want to turn their eyes away from the place they've landed in and be penned up neatly under someone else's orders.

The next thing I remember is the sound of knees and ankles. I wandered away from the house with the idea of getting into another office block, this time a new one with a dirty big field of parking meters blooming over a couple of acres. I had to have a bit of a rest and I haunched down on the kerb when this young girl came along that was like Bee in every way except she was opposite colours.

Some girls are like that, it does them no good in the long run, but you can't talk them out of it. They get all sympathetic when they see dogs with one leg or helpless babies getting bashed or pathetic things like that. That's what made me annoyed with her. She must have jumped to the conclusion that I was helpless, just because I was a little out of breath and needed a rest. To tell you the truth, I was too out of breath to object much, and she ran on and on with this quiet look, and a lot of batting her eyes with sympathy. It was pretty miserable if you could have looked at the scene from a football field away, but you would be making a mistake if you thought I was miserable.

That's a funny thing; the old man used to talk about how crook things were when there was no money, but I've had no money and I got along all right. You get hungry, that's natural, but it's not the end of the world. Old people grumble too much, it's like they thought they should be getting breakfast in bed all their lives and they found that wasn't so; they get very nasty about how the world treats them. I think people should be tougher.

If I could have squeezed a tear out of my face, or got down in the mouth, this nice girl would have stayed with me like a dog for years. You got the feeling about her that as long as you came up to the specification she had in her head, you could walk all over her and it'd be apples with her. She was sort of pre-set, a machine set for a certain mixture of sadness and sympathy, ready to go full ahead if all the coins dropped.

Why is it no one in this world is straight enough to see they don't amount to anything? Pretty soon she left me. I felt good that I'd beaten her soppy kindness.

I felt pretty cheerful. I looked up at the sky, it was wonderful to be alive. For a moment. But in a minute it was gone. Presently I noticed a man with a fruit stall on bicycle wheels. He could move it round without much noise. When I saw him come round the block the second time I started to feel the old alarm buzzing away in my head. He was one of the jokers that were after me, I could tell.

I got back home and all the way home I was thinking of Bee, how the skin on her little finger was a light pink, a sort of sweetness-pink that went right through you.

Stevo was out, so I waited. I wanted to hear more of that old bird story. There was something in me that said if I didn't go after him and get the story I would never know it. Bee said if I waited he would come. I waited.

He came by a couple of thousand years later with a girl called Diana, they were on a horse each. The horses belonged to Diana. I was going to call out to him, Hey! I didn't know you could ride a horse! But it never seemed the right moment to call out. They looked good; Stevo looked as if he was born on a horse's back. They came closer until I could see the veins on the horses' legs and round their eyes.

They leaned inwards to each other, they must have been talking kid talk. The horses' heads leaned inwards, till they touched. But Stevo and his girl looked otherwhere, not at me.

15
SWIMMING POOL

After old Stevo was gone, I sat in the ceiling for three days. I thought of all the stealing and bashing I'd done for him and I wished I'd done more; I wished there were a hundred hours in the day so I could be out clobbering for Stevo and the others. I'd like to be able to say that in those three days I went through a transformation; perhaps I did, but if so, I can't tell the difference. I've become what I've become.

All I can remember of sitting up there, apart from feeling that the whole world had left me, is what Chris said to Bee about the birds. I taught them to leave a hose through a low branch of the jacaranda so a dribble of water came out on a flat rock; the birds drank there and the kids tore up slices of bread and scattered the pieces over the grass for the sparrows, starlings, peewits and robins, silvereyes, currawongs, magpies, kookas and stray jays.

'Mummy, have they got souls?'

'No, dear. All they've got is breadcrumbs.' And that about summed up my life.

When you sit down for a long time, not lying down or weakening at all, you start to feel as I did. It's very clever of humans and all the other boned animals to have solid bones to hold their flesh apart, otherwise we'd all be squashy lumps. That's looking at it in a grateful light; actually my bones wanted to come out through the thin tough skin of my backside after about a day, but I managed to beat my skin and my silly bones, mainly by hating them. And making them do what I wanted.

You'd expect three days of meditation would produce more than that in the way of what I thought I ought to do about things, and what I meant to do about the kids. Something...Instead, nothing. Three days of it.

I didn't feel I ought to stay up there like that. Bee might worry and start to get hard on the kids.

Do you ever have something happen in your head? With me it's usually my eyes. Suddenly I have this shift of vision, as if my eyes were switched off, then they turn on again, but a bit to the left, or lower down. It's the break between that gets me, as if I fell, myself. It's like when your eyes slip down off someone you're about to hammer. I think it's when you feel so hating at your victim while your hand is about to bash forward, but just before it lands. You know, the little disconnection in your head as if your eyes rolled back in to look in your own brain; you have to focus sharply unless you want your hit to go astray and not hurt. Thinking about

185

it, I reckon it's most when you're going to hit someone you're a lot superior to. I remember the same feeling when you kill an animal; only then, of course, you've got the extra spit and the round, easy feeling in your stomach. When I'm talking about is just when it's in your eyes, and there's no one in front of you that you're going to knock over. It just comes when you're walking along or when you stop to remember something.

They could easily stamp out kids like me. But no one's fair dinkum. If they got all the other kids good and nice and sober and industrious, the bottom would fall out of a lot of their rotten trade and shops and promotion. Even if they did it, they'd never know what makes us tick, it's too simple for them to take notice of. They don't get the idea we're simply against them. Whatever they do.

Not everyone can be like me. Most of the kids get round in packs; they like the warm feeling of the others sharing some of the blame if they get caught. They don't develop the metal in the guts that makes you able to do what you like on your own. No one with you, no mates to rat on you, no one with different ideas to foul up good plans.

I was walking along near some land the speculators were going to chop up and plant houses on. I looked at it to fix it in my head in case I ever came that way later when streets and houses were there and I could say to myself I remember what it was like without the changes. It was a flat place, an old watercourse when only the blacks were there, the last place around to be cut up. There was an acre

186

or two of dry, flax-shaped grass, brittle grass and green and brown ferns. You always see green and brown ferns together; the ones that are dying are standing right beside the young growing ones. The dryness and the sound they made of sneaky whispering, hit straight at me. I felt right away all empty and rustling and dry inside.

I knew the cure. A year ago when I was picking up a few clues on photography at a camera club I got to know a woman called Christine. No relation to our Chris. So I got her on the phone and we went to Adams' in town for a few drinks and a bit of a feed. She ordered up very big on the drinks and I ended up taking home to her place all sorts of bottles; beer and wine and even a bottle of whisky. I spent the weekend there and I could hardly get her away from a bottle all the time, but I can't complain, because I was wrecked. She really gave me a good time. It was worth the money the drinks cost me. This was at Mosman, at her house. Around nightfall on the Sunday I heard the phone ring, though she had adjusted the bell so it rang very quietly, and when I sneaked round to listen I heard her making arrangements with another bloke. Sure enough, after she had asked me what time I was going she made a call herself and mentioned a time a quarter hour after the time I told her. Which was eight o'clock. Ten past eight I was still there, to see what she'd do, and sure enough she was edging me to the door.

'You're trying to unload me,' I said.

'You said eight,' said she. 'I'm so tired.'

I was so tired, I went. On the steps outside, I passed a big bloke, a lot older than me, and he was struggling with

187

a cardboard carton full of bottles. She had a capacity, that one. Must have had a gullet like a horse collar.

With a weekend of breath and staleness and the smell of bedsheets, I got a powerful wish for some trees around me, instead of potted plants. The seats in the stand down at the oval weren't too bad for a bed. Next day I walked down to the swimming hole at the back of Cheltenham; running was out, I was so tired, and it was a good day for a swim. I stayed there all day, someone bright had put a rope from a tree so you could swing out over the water and drop in. That was nice, until at the top of one of my swings I looked out over the hanging rock and saw a man and a woman in the ferns. They didn't care about snakes, and it was getting on to snake weather.

I didn't want to have to see people doing that wherever I went, so I left. They saw me, though, they were watching me. I gave them a few good swings, to show off a bit, but they weren't a bit embarrassed. I could have made things hot for them if I'd wanted to, but this time I let them off; I didn't even want them to know for sure I'd seen them. The main thing is to look innocent; that's all they know—what they see.

I wished I'd gone to the Jungo, that's west of the old slaughter yards, even if the place was lousy with Estonians potting away at kookaburras with twenty-twos, getting something for lunch. At least there'd be no one near when you went in, or trying to talk to you. If there's one thing gives me the tom-tits it's people talking to you. I don't mean if you ask them something, but when they just come up and talk to you for no reason at all. I never answer.

In a way, though, I liked the idea of those two being down by the hole on a Monday, at least they weren't pretending to be necessary to the country's trade-health. I've read a magazine or two, there's enough machines now to do all the work, but people just aren't used to the idea of the streets being full of people. They like to be safely clocked in.

I reckon I'll never get used to the ideas you're supposed to have when you're old. I stayed down in the bush, it was very pleasant with a bit of breeze coming up the track to meet you, but I did no running that day either, I was just too hot. The new bark skins on the young gums reminded me of the pole vault sticks we used to cut when I was young. I had a friend years ago, Bongo. Bongo had a cousin that admired pole-vaulters, she said; we got her in his lounge room on Sundays when she was down on a visit and his parents were at church, but I didn't like kissing her after he'd had a go, so I always got in first.

In those days we used to swim at the slaughter yards, we were there the day it was a hundred and eighteen, naked in the water. The Fishies was a better pool, deeper and cooler. I was lying flat on a grey rock then, and the sound of my fingers on the stone startled me, it took me back immediately to the sound my fingers made when I tried to ease my brother's toy shark away from him. Why did they give all the presents to him? Did they like him? But he was always grumbling, there were tears in his eyes half the time and a miserable look. Frowns, yells. And I was all sunshine. Our stupid grandmother gave him that overcoat, none for me. Why should I forget that? Life's too short to forget those things.

189

And when I got home that Sunday to Bay Road to ask the old man what that word meant that the man wrote on his friend's back, I was the one that had to run. The Papworths used to stone you going to school and coming home, there was a quarry opposite their house; I always meant to go back when I got older and land a few on them, but I never did. Their biggest brother could swim for miles under water, I used to think, there was no limit to what big kids could do. I suppose I knew all along it would be my brother who would get picked on by my cousins and tossed in the water; he was always miserable. We were little then.

Billycart races, swimming in Hen and Chicken Bay, I remember it all. That's the sort of life I intended to have; it's what I like.

Stevo was sick about this time and I bunked most of the time in the roof of the dressing sheds at the swimming pool. The new one near home. It was easy to get back home in the daytime to look in on them and give Bee a hand. I tried to let Stevo get away with more little things than he was usually allowed, I knew that would help to build his confidence.

He broke the only paint brush we had and went round asking, 'Where's the wig of it?' He was getting better.

Chris was starting to take an interest in 'Mummy's toots', and went round with tennis balls in her dress. She pricked up her ears when she heard about Auntie Jane having a baby.

'Has Jane had the baby yet or is it still muckin' round in her tummy?'

I dug up an old mouth organ and let Chris play it,

since Stevo had got one from the woman next door for his birthday. But with Chris you had to explain. We'd just been talking about my brother that died and what we said must have stuck in her head. We'd got some of his things from the flat where he lived, each one in the family took what he wanted. Chris knew her own mouth organ once belonged to yet another brother and couldn't understand how we could have got it and given it to her if the other brother wasn't dead too.

'If Paul isn't dead, how'd you get the mouth organ?'

Stevo had a dream when he was getting better. 'I saw some men last night getting old. And their heads falling off. Right off.' And soon he started eating again. I used to bring him paper bags of chipped potatoes, since Bee didn't like you giving them lollies.

'I like chipped potatoes. I think they're so nourishing.' I even started taking them all for walks round the street and down to the running park and the swings. When I went down one street instead of another, he said, 'You said you were going that way, but your eyes were very mysterious, so I knew you were going to go this way.' I had seen a man leaning against a dark car, and I thought I knew him from somewhere. It wouldn't have been good, if I'd really known him, for him to see me with the kids, for if he wanted to cut me down or anything he would have known right away where my weak spot was, and how to hurt me. Actually I recalled later that it was a man called Moey, that I saw last at a circus riding a goat for a kewpie doll prize.

The baker up there still had one cart going with a horse. It was cheaper and he wanted to use the horse rather than sell it to the knacker's. I'd told Stevo about horses and knackers and when he saw old Barnsie's animal, he said, 'That's a gluey sort of horse.' I didn't really know if they still use them for glue, but that's what I told him.

Later, I borrowed a car from the car park outside the station, a Holden—you can get into them very easily—and we were both very satisfied, Bee and me, to see how he was almost his old self again. He took with him the underwater goggles I got for him and stared and made noises out the car window at the drivers and walking workers we passed.

'With this noise I'll stop their minds.' He was getting eager to grow up, and this I wasn't very keen on.

'Grown-ups have such fun. Or do they?' he remarked. I hoped he'd stay a boy as long as he could. I tried to. It was good to be out driving with Bee and the kids, like a real family. Chris sang for us her special song, she'd started to go to school. 'Way down yonder in the paw-paw patch,' but what she sang was, 'Lay down yonder in the paw-paw patch.' You couldn't get her to change it, either. Bee tried to.

Sitting up there driving someone else's car, I thought of the old man sitting up in his bed at the Randwick TB hospital and how I visited him once in three years and how on the night he died and I slept there, all I could think of was the noise of his dying had stopped and I was relieved.

We got to Coal and Candle Creek on the road that the old man had helped build and I think some people there might have thought they recognised the car we were in, because an old man with grey in his hair came up to us, with a question on the tip of his tongue. I could see that, so I took a sudden quick step towards him. He made the same back move that young Stevo had made when the water hit his leg. No one else seemed to see what nearly happened, he went away, and since he probably didn't say anything to the people he was with before he came over, he didn't have to explain anything about his sudden retreat.

I played with the kids and got them iceblocks and things, and made plenty of time having lunch, hoping Stevo might get round to telling me his story of the Chantic Bird. He didn't. I didn't want to be at him all the time, pestering for a story. Besides, who was the kid? Him or me?

At night when I got back to the swimming pool sheds, I fell asleep on my back and had another coloured dream. This time it was black. Three tall black men standing in front of me with creases in their faces, like tribal markings, only these were fresh cut in their faces with a knife. The sides of the cuts had sharp edges, like a razor cut makes and the funny thing was that although the wounds were red inside, there was no blood leaking over the sharp sides of the cuts.

It was a weird dream, for the black men didn't do anything. They just stood there, looking straight forward, not even at me, as if into their future. Only I knew you can't look into the future. Just standing still and watching, and the cuts red and fresh. All you can see is the past.

The sound of a kid rasping on the metal of the wire fence woke me and I could hear whoever it was walking in rubber shoes on the old concrete path. Then I got on to a man with a spike picking up papers in the park part, ready for another day of kids and lollies. There was something about him I couldn't stand, he was too like the other ones that kept bobbing up ready to chase me off from wherever I wanted to get settled. I couldn't take the chance on him not being dangerous to me, so I climbed down and got out.

They might just as well send the whole population after me. After all, I'm against the lot of them.

I kept sitting there in the car and waiting, but Bee was a long time coming out. Didn't they want a ride? This time I'd got a big white American car for them and I'd only be able to have it until the people got back on the train from Sydney; I wouldn't like the family to be in the car when I got picked up for borrowing it.

That day I just couldn't wait. I told myself I'd come back later, but right now I had to keep moving. You know, there's a madness in the air; all you have to do is reach up and grab a bit of it. And when you do, it works for you.

You know, all I seem to do is steal. I was thinking about that as the big Chev floated over the bitumen, in and out the traffic. Now and again some birds would play with the car, flying low out from the footpaths and swooping almost under the wheels. The fact that they were laughing at me and the car and anyone that couldn't get off the ground, didn't even annoy me. But behind their little games you could see that they would have been very serious if they'd been a ton or two bigger. Instead of dive-bombing the windscreen or the front tyres, they would have carried the whole lot away, and digested me and it at their leisure. The wagtails were skites, their speed seemed to vary when they came from the side, it made it look as if they knew they had everything covered, and I must tell you I was waiting for one of them to swoop past me and go under an oncoming wheel. Or better still, for them to miss another car and for me to get them under my wheels, or splat against the windscreen.

I felt sort of sarcastic inside myself, as if I wanted to twist my mouth at the world and keep it twisted. Moments like that it would be easy to ease the wheel a fraction to the right and keep your eyes open right up to the crash. I drew a couple of circles with my hands—with the steering wheel inside them—and headed back to the house. Bee and the kids were waiting, which was a better situation.

Talking to them came hard, the way I felt. There was right through me a sort of anger or madness, I could feel it warming me inwards from the skin, it made my bones feel more lively—they wanted to jump about in their smooth coverings of gristle and muscle—but I knew if I let them, they would only flail round and hit whoever was nearest, and that was the family. I must never hurt the family.

No sooner said to myself than forgotten. What happened I don't know. Only that somewhere along the Gosford road the ferment inside me boiled over. It has always fascinated me that all you have to do to crash is move that wheel a fraction to the right and it's head-on with another car, or to the left and it takes longer off the road. Just a tiny movement. And you're in control of it. No one else. I made the movement.

To the left. Whump and off the road, the ground fell away but not too sharply and the wheels didn't slip much and it was through the trees, missing them—not yet—it was easy enough to go straight for a soft bark red gum or a peeling old stringybark, over a couple of saplings, tasting the moment, spinning it out. Then Bee pushed some words out. She was gripping the seat, but she made no attempt to hang onto me. Now that I think of it, I'm not real pleased.

The words didn't come out crazed or anything. She had her panic inside and kept it there.

'If you want to kill us all, why don't you get a gun?' And that was one of the cruellest things she could have said. Somehow the feeling inside me had gone away and for a moment I was surprised at the contents of the last minute and what I'd almost done. I put the lid on that, though; I didn't want to be feeling guilt. You can't drive properly when you're guilty. So I took the car over a pretty big bump so that everyone hit their heads on the car roof and the kids thought it was great fun. It surprised me they weren't scared.

The owner would be surprised to see tree bark on his bumpers. Some people looked when I put the car back, so Bee told me, but I reckoned it was only because people like us got out of it. We must have looked a pretty young family.

197

I was putting the car back in the line-up outside the railway station where all the commuters parked to save themselves walking a mile there and back every day. The original parking spot was gone but the one I found was only a few dozen yards away.

When I got out and finished wiping the marks off the wheel and windows and seats, there he was. Petersen, I mean. It was his car I'd been using. That's how I met him. I walked home with him to see where he lived. It was the big old house with the guava trees: when I delivered for old Cowan the grocer, the old lady used to give me a feast of fruit there. In the yard they had a summer house with six sides. That was where I used to meet him to put my story down on paper when his girl friend wasn't playing the violin there.

I didn't go home with Bee and the kids, I went out looking for a car of my own. I wanted one to live in for a while; it seemed to me I had been wasting my time living like a rat in other people's buildings and all over the place. With a car you could get around. It might be necessary to change the plates every couple of weeks, because that was the time it took for a complaint to be processed and the narks to get out looking for you. The best thing to do was what I did. A kid that I used to go to school with was in the car business; you know, getting in, shorting the ignition, driving up the backboard of his big covered trailer and dropping it in one of his farm sheds out in the cow and citrus country, with spray guns and the works. He used to do a proper job, only a prang and a few fractures would show it up when the police got nosey about the engine number or the chassis.

He'd do anything: change wheels, put in new engines, a new paint job or even only a slight paint difference, like a stripe or a different coloured top. I didn't want him knowing what I was doing, so I went out on the Singleton road to one of his sheds and rolled one away that he'd finished and took with me a heap of rego plates so he wouldn't know exactly which plates I was using at any time and wouldn't be able to turn me in with a nasty phone call.

It was pleasant, living in a nice big car, and I made the most of it; joy-riding, picking up money for food and petrol outside the pubs from middle-aged drunks: it was a neat way to live. I had to pick a quiet place to stop and sleep, otherwise someone else like me might clobber me at night. I slept light and got a few hours down in the daytime, so I wasn't wearing myself out. I still felt the itch often to turn that wheel a fraction to the right, but I guess I never meant it, because I'm still here telling you about it. I saw some pretty things, driving around. I passed a car with a few kids like myself in it, only they had girls in too. I knew the sort of girls, not like Bee at all. This lot were so used to life that the girl in front who was doing something to the kid that was driving, was talking to her friend in the back seat, who was performing likewise with the boy in the back. I suppose it was a day off for them, unless they had picked on my way of living. Their parents probably thought they were staying at a friend's place, maybe, but what was more like it was their parents probably knew very well what they were doing and envied them. Very few adult people have done all the dirty things they'd like to have done. The ones I've seen are chock-a-block with regret for the lives they haven't led, the sheilas they haven't raped, the tills they haven't robbed, the murders they haven't done, the sex they haven't had. They were too honest to try to stop their kids doing the things they would have done if only they'd been game enough. Somewhere along the line they gave up, and tried to please someone else or keep their job or stay out of trouble. They're failures. You can't stay out of trouble and still live as you want. The important thing is not to care what other people think, specially police and people in uniforms. Even if the uniform is only a white shirt and collar and tie.

It was good driving on weekdays. The streets were pretty clear of citizens. Only blokes with jobs were out. And people like me. I was surprised to see so many people like me out in cars, mostly older, but what they were doing was just the same. Somehow I didn't like that; I'd rather have been the only one to think of it and then I would have kept it dark.

I suppose some of the things I did were a bit young, like smashing. The sound of things smashing gets me. It makes me feel easy and warm in my chest. One of my favourites, apart from tossing things off a height, was to carry a supply of bottles in the car and toss them out and cause a sensation. Not at people. At least not often. I shot one at a man that was belting a dog. I couldn't care less about dogs, but ordinary people say you shouldn't hurt animals, unless you're going to eat them, so why shouldn't I keep this man to what he ought to do? It was a sensation, that one. The bottle didn't hit him, it hit the dog. Only a glancing blow, and then flew off the dog's back onto the headlights of a car. The bottle smashed and ginger ale bubbled everywhere and the headlights smashed. The owner wasn't there, but several people near the shops took the car number and wrote down a description of the man, maybe, or even his name—he could have been a local—and hurried off to the row of public phones to ring the papers or the police or the RSPCA or the man's wife or boss or neighbours or church, anywhere they could dob him in. The ones that couldn't get to the public phones rang up from shop phones. They all thought he'd tried to bottle the dog. I slowed down when I saw no one had noticed me. There was only one citizen that tackled the man head on and that was an old lady from last century; she didn't realise that until the copper got there the bloke might do anything. As it was, he went to shove her away, but she lurched a bit in the ordinary way of walking and he missed. You couldn't have much respect for last century, though, because as soon as she stopped castigating the man, she walked across the road without looking, as if the world owed her a life, and everyone was going to stop so as not to take hers. Maybe her yelling at the man was as much out of tune as the way she crossed the road. Fancy thinking she had rights on the road when cars were doing fifty all round her. I had stopped the car and reversed, because that was the natural thing to do these days; no one goes by an accident or a fight; everyone stops to gape. I gaped and the old woman stepped right in front of me when I started off again. I threw out the anchors and hit the horn but there was another surprise. Someone had fitted the car with a two-note screamer and the blast from the horn lifted her off her feet. Unfortunately, it lifted her right on to my front bumpers. The circus started again, and the people who hadn't finished their phone calls reporting the man and the dog were in a fever to get me included too. She untangled herself and I got away, but just in case they reported me with the right car number, I changed plates a few miles on and bought a roll of red sticky tape from a paper shop and stuck it in two strips on both sides of the car. You'd be surprised how a little thing like a red stripe changes the look of anything.

I had a funny experience when I took the car into the city. I left the car down near the Opera House and went up on the highest of the new buildings. I don't want to tell you too much, only that I took a little hot Japanese Grand Prix transistor with me—people don't worry if they see a kid with a radio going, they know he's harmless—and there I stood up on the top looking over the city. If you were average height you'd have trouble looking over, but I'm pretty tall. I remember thinking when I looked over Sydney that it'd be a great feeling to own a city, you have a lot of those ants and bugs—the cars looked like bugs from there—in the palm of your hand. But just then, in the middle of a programme they had on called Mourning Melody, they stopped and this man came on with a quiet voice, the sort of voice that is thinking you'll go away if it gets any louder, and what do you think it was saying?

Cast yourself down. That hit me. I switched the thing off right away and looked straight down. This time it was a voice telling me; back in the car with Bee and the kids there wasn't any voice, only something in me making me almost

202

do it. I don't usually think hard about anything, but this time I did. I tried to concentrate away from the voice on to the height of the building, the pretty houses on the north bank of the river, the trains like worms crawling across the coathanger. And down on to the sails of the Opera House, blown ashore in a strong wind, beached and too heavy to push off again, like a helpless houseboat rigged for the America's Cup.

As usual, when I ignored the thought for long enough to pass through the action stage, it lost power and left me. I didn't jump. That day I invented a brilliant new method of stealing. I called it the blitz-steal. The idea was to hit a shop very fast and be on the run before they'd seen you, or very soon after. And I worked out a special camouflage, you could call it the before and after. You had to look different behind from what you did in front. I got an old jumper and painted it red behind—it was black in front—and put a big number on it in white. My hair I made lighter behind with some flour and I made the heels of my shoes different with a different polish. All set.

I knocked off a couple of transistors from an electrical shop in Crow's Nest, but there was no kick in it. No buzzard saw me. There was no chase. The trick was to park your car half a mile away to give you time to get away so they couldn't catch up enough to see the number while you were starting it. I got rid of the electrical stuff in pubs. It's easy to part people from their cash when they've had a few. I got in supplies of food like that, too. You go in a self-service, preferably with trolleys with detachable tops, then when you're ready for the girl on the cash desk, leave it in the wire

203

basket, put it on the desk, and when the woman in front has moved out of the way to get her goods packed in a bag, lift out something you don't want, like a leg of months old lamb and drop it at the feet of the cash girl in the little space she has. She'll try to pick it up and that's where you beat it.

They call out and yell a lot, but no one will stop you. Citizens have no guts. It's all the better if you roll up a white apron under your jumper, already tied round your waist, so you can pull it down in front when you're getting out. They always think you have to work in a shop if you wear an apron. That's where people get trapped because of their always thinking in the same way, they get habits of thinking, they learn to recognise things like aprons and different colours and they think they've got the keys of the kingdom. To trick them, all you have to use is their own habits.

I had a joker follow me once that could run. I don't think I'd have got away even if I hadn't been carrying a basket of groceries. That was at Hurstville. In the end I slowed down, exhausted practically, making straight for two old ladies. I tried to time it so he would reach me just as we reached the old ladies. They looked up and smiled; no one ever thinks you're going to crash into them; and I sidestepped. This runner bloke hit them halfway down and carried them about five yards. This time some bystanders took a hand and started kicking this fellow, mainly because he was flat on the ground with two old ladies on top of him. When he started to get up they got back out of reach, which was prudent, because he was as big as me. I was long gone, and the car started at the first touch, mainly because

204

I look at the points and clean them every day and test every single electrical contact in the circuit. I believe in making a car work for me, but also in keeping it in good condition so that it can.

I remember driving away from that little scene and sweating. The water out of me came down the back of my neck and when I put up my hand to feel it, the hairs on my head were all wet. I just couldn't help thinking of something Stevo had said when we were in the car. After I'd toyed with the idea of suiciding us all.

He was in the back seat looking over me, at my hair.

'I can see bottom, Mum,' he said. She didn't answer, she was still fairly rigid, sitting there. That was after I'd gone off the road.

I thought about that all the time I was driving away. And I thought about Bee. So much so that I started thinking about women in general.

Have you ever gone into the hi-jacking business? I don't mean with a car full of other slobs, so that there's a dozen mouths to squeal. I mean by yourself. You only have to say Pass the straws in a milk bar and you can be onto something. Or, Hey Billie Jean, which way to Ostracise? If she stops to say Where? you're in. The best one I had was a girl a bit older than me, about nineteen, and she told me where to go. To Balmoral Island. You know that little spit of land in the middle of Balmoral Beach? There. At night it can be very romantic, but this was broad daylight. I wouldn't have if she hadn't insisted. It's my natural instinct against doing things in the open. What finished me with her was

I swore once. She was very sexy, but if you swore that was bad. Very bad. She was so loud about it that I took her back home across the Bridge and on the middle of it I stopped and pushed her out.

Have you ever seen someone on foot in the middle of the Bridge? If she hadn't been pretty she'd be there now. As it turned out, she got picked up before I was off the Bridge. I waited and watched and she was in with four kids. They were taking no notice of her, working up to it inside themselves in silence. I reckon I knew what would happen to her, the only thing in doubt was where; if she was lucky they wouldn't take her as far as National Park. There's something tempting about being in the bush, it makes you think you can do what you like. The only hard work you have to do is dig a hole for the body.

It's a mistake to think people know how bad your intentions are; when I got home again Bee didn't hold it against me that I tried to kill them all; what she held against me was that I had pulled her leg in a pretty dangerous way, but she didn't mention the danger to the kids. She said she trusted my driving and I wouldn't take them into any danger I couldn't get them out of. Then she asked me about the car. That was the first time she ever talked about the cars I took them out in.

I told her I shut the car and put everything back where it was so the fuzz would know it was only a temporary steal if anyone reported it. The car I got from Russo's was outside, and I had come in wearing my leather coat. You could sleep in it, and it was warm.

'Dad, I hate to tell you this,' said Stevo, 'but burglars wear them!'

'I am the burglar,' I said with menace, spreading my arms like they do in the horror films. Somehow I expected him to be as scared of one as of the other. The kids liked scary things. Bee got him off that subject by showing me his latest homework.

'Show Daddy the kangaroo and the lion.' He got out his little exercise book with the salmon cover and showed me.

'Read it to Daddy,' she said.

'The kangaroo and the lion. Once while a lion was eating in the jungle he heard a noise. It was the kangaroo in the bushes. The kangaroo sprang at him. After that they were friends.' He stopped, Bee clapped, I thought it was colossal. Actually it was. There was a little kid searching in his brain for words about animals, and finding some. They didn't make all that much sense, but they were words from inside him.

I was so pleased I helped Bee get them to bed, then out to my mobile cave to drive round a bit. In a car you carry your own darkness with you at night, you can see out better than anyone can see in. I slept parked on the driveway of a service station, you'd think it was just a car left there for sale. The next day I got Bee to keep the kids home from school and come for a good long drive. They had their coloured pencils and books in case they got bored. I got the idea of allowing them to decorate the inside of the car, too, with their paints. It was easy enough as long as I didn't go to town on the brakes or slice the corners too much. Bee didn't like them getting in a mess, but I got her to let them wear their old things, so that was OK.

It would have been a good day only it started to rain. Chris livened things up with her song about 'Lay down yonder in the paw-paw patch'. That was always good for about twenty minutes, but after that the others started to get very restless.

'All the houses look little when it starts to rain,' said Chris, going straight from song to words.

'How many days is it to Christmas?' queried Stevo. I started to answer him when I remembered I didn't have any presents for them. We were going through poor old Lithgow, the people looked cold and miserable in the streets even in December, but the shops were putting on a cheerful show with flags and signs and streamers, trying hard to loosen the last bit of change in the citizens' pockets. A big banner said something religious about Bethlehem.

'Lithgow is a long way from Bethlehem, isn't it Daddy?' I didn't want to tell him how much further I was. I was further still by the time I'd gone to town on one of their sports stores. I got a few little things for Stevo, enough to ease my conscience. I'd have to leave it a bit longer for Chris and Allie. I had to leave them waiting for about an hour while I spied out the streets behind the shops, so as not to make any wrong turnings when the shop workers were after me. It was risky, in a foreign town, but as usual the one who acts first has the initiative. Bee gave me a slight needle when she saw me ditch the things under the boot lid.

'You're starting to find things everywhere.'

She meant before they were lost. She was getting a bit too quick on the eye, and a bit too ready to unlock the tongue.

'You're starting to see things.' I didn't mean it to sound like that, but once it was out, that was it. She sat a bit further away and looked out the other window for long enough to get Stevo in.

He said, 'You mustn't be upset, 'cause Daddy's a friend.' That didn't make any difference to her, but she smiled at the kid. I could see by her face she was having pains and I thought I remembered seeing the grateful way she had sat down when she got into the car. I started to get her talking but all I could think of to say was 'What direction is the last town?' She never knew which direction was which. You could box her up just by going round a corner. It's different with me, I never lose track of where the west and the north are. I don't think south and east, only north and west; I get all my directions that way.

We stopped for eats half a dozen miles outside Lithgow and the kids were so happy playing round near the water— we stopped by a bridge—that I lay on my back and went to sleep.

Sure enough, up came a coloured dream. I was in a boat, finding my way home to port and when I got outside the harbour I radioed my position to the port officials and so on, then I came in the harbour, but I kept getting strange answers to my calls. There I was, in the middle of the stream, and I could see them milling about, getting into boats, coming to look for me. They kept saying, 'Confirm your position', and 'Show yourself', and when

I got them to put a direction finder on my radio signals they had to admit I was where I said I was, but they couldn't see me. That was silly. I repeated everything, so they couldn't possibly make a mistake and they started closing in on me, still saying they couldn't see me. In the end they were right on top of me, aiming everything at me and I was screaming into the radio, 'You must be able to see me, you're right on top of me,' but all they could say was, 'We get your signals, and directionally you're there, but we can't see you'.

And to themselves they said, 'There's nothing there. It's his voice all right, but we've got the finest directionals and the greatest magnification possible in the world, trained right on where the signals come from, but as far as our instruments show, he's not there.'

I was pretty wet when I woke up, apparently I'd been thrashing about in my sleep. Bee looked at me pretty worried, and the kids were playing further away but kept looking back at me. She must have told them to go away.

That was the most embarrassing part, having Bee see me in one of those dreams.

Why did they? Why did a man and a woman get together that particular time just to make something they could be parents to? Why couldn't they have used self-restraint just once? It wasn't worth it, to be alive with Bee looking at me like that, looking and not looking, and the kids looking over their shoulders, with Stevo loyally trying to get Chris to play. Allie was too young to notice, that was the only good thing. She smiled most of the time.

*

In the car Stevo took my mind off my own whys and wherefores by getting involved in mathematics. Numbers seemed to get him.

'The biggest number in the world is a hundred million thousand. You can't have any bigger. You can't go any futher 'cause then there's Pole.'

Don't ask me, I haven't got a clue what Pole is, all I know is he said it with a capital letter. I wish I knew what went on in his head, maybe he was a brain.

'How you getting on at school, Stevo?' I asked.

'All right. I've got a new teacher, though. Miss Thomson.'

'Which you like better, Miss Thomson or Miss Adamson?'

'Miss Thomson, just a twinkle better.'

'Did you tell Miss Thomson you didn't go to the Show?'

'No, I think that would be a very sad thing to say.'

Bee said, 'He was pretty quiet about the Show. The other kids all mentioned it in their compositions.'

That shut me up. I wasn't on deck to take them to the local Shows, either Castle Hill or Parramatta. We ruled out the big one in town, it was too noisy, too crowded and too dirty, Bee said.

The kids went back to their picture books and singing. The next I heard was Bee giving Stevo the rounds of the back seat for saying bugger.

'I'm not saying it to other people, just seeing if I can still say the word.' He was right behind me when he said it, making sure I heard his excuse. He sprayed a circular waterfall when he spoke, and I had a wet neck.

When we stopped at a little store, I gave the kids money to buy something for themselves and you should have seen what a little taste of money did to them. They wouldn't show each other what they bought, as if they would lose a little of it if someone else saw it.

I knew they would never grow up and I hoped so, too. I would never be a mature citizen until I was rigid in my box, and I guess I didn't want them to be, either.

I was so involved with the kids I took a wide corner too fast and nearly collected a country ambulance from Bathurst going like mad back to Sydney with a case the country doctors couldn't handle. The ambulance didn't shift its course on the curve and it was left to me to haul on the wheel enough just to scrape paint.

Bee looked more scared that time than when I really went off the road. She covered up by asking Stevo to tell me the story of the Chantic Bird.

'What story? I don't remember any story,' he replied.

'You know, the one you were telling Daddy.'

'I'll tell him one from my new book,' he said.

'Never mind,' I put in.

'That's not nice, Stevo,' said Bee. 'You know very well what story.'

'Forget it.'

'No. He should do what he said he was going to.'

'Don't go begging the kid for me. He said he's forgotten it, that's good enough for me.'

'I'll let you know if I remember,' he said. It sounded pretty cheeky to me, but what could I do? I never worried about him being cheeky before.

'When I'm bigger I want diamonds,' Chris said suddenly.

'What brought that on?' Bee asked.

'I just heard a lady on the TV say it.'

'She's always wanting something fresh.' That was Stevo. The limelight had been shifted away from him, his sister was coming ahead, fast.

I took them home, all fast asleep in the car. I didn't mind going out of my way to do something for them, they were as good as my own kids. But I started to think the best way to look after them all might be to stay away and send money. They'd soon forget me; there's not much to remember.

I parked the car outside the house that night and slept in it. It was a bit like guarding the family. Next morning a kid I used to know made a point of pretending to pass by and when he got to the point he wanted me to come in with him tapping a petrol line down on the Parramatta where it comes across from a big refinery under the river to feed the tanks of another oil company and across some open ground to the tanks of a third company. He told me his method of getting into the line and I wiped him right away. Not only because I would never go in with someone else, but because I thought of a better way of tapping the line, while he was talking. I'd better not tell you too much about it, but my way made no noise, caused no sparks and took half a day, using acid. This kid would probably have got into the top of the line and had the stuff spraying all over the place. The time to get it was when they weren't pumping and you could

213

tell that by putting your ear to it. Then when you had your own half-inch line tapped in, all you had to do was fill your drums in the mangroves and float them out.

I got rid of this kid and he went away mumbling about how I'd change when I saw him in his eighty-guinea suits. There was no sense answering him, but I told myself I'd change when I was good and ready. They weren't going to change me. I was incorrigible. Just the same I didn't like letting him off altogether, going away muttering and me not doing anything to cure him of the habit. It gave me a bad feeling not to get even.

Once when I was a kid the old man, who was a very excitable type, was excitable in the wrong company and got bashed up. That was in a vacant block on Parramatta Road along from the Saleyards pub. I got even for him. That's what I believe in—revenge. Getting even. The man that did most of the kicking at the old man, I waited for him the day I turned fifteen and a half, it was a Saturday, I had to follow him far as the railway to get a chance to do him. He got off the train before it had stopped and ran before slowing down. I didn't let him slow down, I ran alongside him and pushed him off the other edge of the platform. There was no train coming the other way, lucky for him, but he was messed up a lot. When they get over forty they can't take knocks.

As I walked back along the platform, I casually eased my knife out of my pocket so that the metal of it shone in the sun. The workers in the train made no move. The public's got no guts, they need leaders and bosses and things to lean on.

Inside the house there was a small emergency. Stevo had kicked over the traces and Bee had to strip him and give him a going-over with a whippy stick. The smell of breakfast got me into the house and I came in on the end of the argument. I tried to say something oily to calm them both down, but they both snapped at me. At least Stevo snapped at me; I only felt that Bee did, she didn't actually say anything.

I gave Stevo a whack that was not well judged and he had to pick himself off the skirting board. He went away and when we went to look for him we found a note but no Stevo.

It read; 'Sorry I will never ever come back, again, good by for ever. Sine Stevo. It is realy, that is a finish. You don't like me, do you.'

Bee was still watering at the eyes when I left to look for him. I tracked him a little way by his shoes, where he walked over the dew on the grass, and finally ran him to earth under a low-spreading tree outside a neighbour's house. He hadn't run far and I only caught him from the sound of a plastic glass of pineapple drink against the tree trunk. He wanted to run away and he'd taken his supplies, but already they were half finished and he was only two hundred yards from home.

There was nothing I could have said to him on the way back, it was just as well I left it to Bee; she only needed a couple of words to poor old Stevo and he was in tears and burying his face in her lap. If she spoke to you in the language of the Watutsi or in Estonian you'd want to kiss the words as they floated in the air. That's how her voice was.

215

The sight of a man in a sort of uniform straightened me up a bit, you know how I hate uniforms. But it was only a service-station dress; it was a man I knew that used to go around damaging people's cars then turning up in time to recommend them to his mate, who had a panel-beating business. He either hit a car with the heel of his hand and pushed in a panel, or scraped the paint off with an ornament he had on his key-ring. It was made of stainless steel and the scrape it left looked like a brush with another car. Something about the way he looked at the car made me prick up my suspicions. I decided to get out of there; it was just as likely that he might dob me in to the coppers just to get a good mark for himself.

I drove away eating potato chips, thinking to myself I was making a hole in space, through and through the vastness of the daytime that covered the hemisphere, imagining that if I could keep the car going straight, I could get it in a gradual climb off the surface of the earth and end up aimed right away from this planet. A kid on a bike, lairising, leaned right over in front of me, a pedal touched the ground, and he went ass over tip right in front of me. If he hadn't rolled over as soon as he hit, he would have been minced because I didn't move the wheel a fraction. It reminded me of a game we used to play, throwing sticks out of someone's car, aiming them between the spokes of bikes and watching the riders hitting the dirt. Or the concrete.

When I stopped for gasoline at the green and gold sign of one of the oil companies involved in what I said before about the business of using the same product, some older kids told me they had a good thing going in stolen

216

cars—they looked at mine very close—but presently a fellow bowled up, better dressed than them and it turned out here was another leader. Leader! I told them what they could do with leaders.

Just then there was the sound of a car behind me. I thought they might have signalled a passing prowl car and had it pull in behind me, but I was lucky. I listened a bit more and it turned out to be a little fall of water in some underground pipes, under the driveway. I don't think the others heard it. I've got ears like a wild cat.

I ditched the car and went back home. There were too many people knew me, too many kids trying to get me in with them. There was only one place I felt comfortable.

By this time I had something in mind for Petersen, so I let him worm it out of me that Stevo and the kids weren't my little brother and sisters but my kids and Bee's. Mine as far as I knew, anyway, because at one stage she had the bad luck to be initiated up behind the factories in Duffy Avenue. I say I had something in mind, because by this time my own story seemed to be his. He treated it as his, he was getting inside all my secrets and I had started to feel he was like one of those men that had been following me. He might even be the most dangerous of them.

That's why I've kept a lot back. That's why I didn't tell him the truth about the kids. When I told him those lies, I could see he was more curious than ever, his skinny frame jerked with anticipation of more secrets to come.

When I got back home to Bee she had her head on a pillow, sick.

217

17

HOUSE

Some things are easy to remember. The cab I had was a
real old Mercedes diesel, they have a few of them round
Parramatta and I was on my way to the house and no one
there. Bee had taken the kids with her to the Entrance for
two weeks of the holidays. She told me she would be back in
time for Christmas, she liked to be home for Christmas. It
was pretty luxurious taking a cab, and you can bet I didn't
stay in it right up to the door. Right where the pedestrian
crossing is in Bee's suburb the cab stopped for old Miss
Jones—that was the old lady that made a lifework of taking
in stray kids—to stagger across and when he was about to
go, with a line of traffic behind him and a line in front so
he couldn't turn right, I whipped the door open and hopped
out. It was just that part of the day when the light is going
and the dark is almost enough for cars to switch on their

lights, which they are very reluctant to do. I was down the railway path and round behind the shopping centre and across the road before the driver could turn the car. If he'd been quicker and speeded up when he saw me go for the door, he'd have got me, but people are too kindhearted; they pull back from hurting you just when they could have you on a plate.

It was dark enough when I got home; it was silly to have neighbours see you when there was no need. The house smelled dark, like a cave, inside.

Sitting in there alone and all the bad things I'd ever done started to rise up in front of my eyes. I grinned in the dark over most of them, but not about scalding Stevo, or taking their friends from the others, and not about leaving the old man alone for three years in hospital or Ma when she was dying for six months, or even my young brother that died. Next to Stevo, that one that died was on my conscience about the most. Although Ma and the old man had a pretty rotten go, too. Ma used to try to get us to think he was the finest man on earth. I hope no one ever talks like that about me.

I sort of wandered into Bee's room and somehow it turned out that I got into her old papers and souvenirs. Not that I mucked them up or anything; I put them back in place exactly where I found them, but there were bundles of letters, piles of old programmes, crumpled handkerchiefs with old smears on, train tickets with the sleeper butts still on, all sorts of things. I pulled the shades and rigged up a barricade so I could put a light on without being seen from outside. It was more comfortable then. There were a couple of things that made me a bit uneasy, things like other kids' writings on her old theatre tickets; she'd been to the ballet with some joker from the Glebe a few times. I didn't know she ever went to places like that, she never ever said a word about ballet to me. It's amazing how close-mouthed women can be. But the worst thing about it was thinking I hardly knew her. She'd done things and been places I'd never know about.

When I got to one particular letter I read it twice, put it and the rest of the things back in the drawer, all in order, put out the light and took away the barricade and went out to a place a few streets away. It was dark and quiet; my sort of night. They had a dog, but it was too sound asleep to hear me. They also had a back porch and since it was a hot night the back door was open; this kid slept on the back verandah, it was one of those old places with the old verandah closed in. Not too different from our house. I clubbed this kid good and proper. He would be doing other things besides writing love letters when he woke up in the morning.

I realise he would probably never know who did it or why, but I'm not the kind of person that has to worry about those points. As long as I do what I want to, that's all that is on my mind. I never liked that kid, he was the sort that slapped you on the back and said merry things while watching you closely. Maximum impact, but meaning nothing except watch him closely.

'What would you do if I asked you to sleep with me,' Petersen used to ask. He expected me to say Punch you in the nose, and I did. He had got to the stage where he thought he knew all about me, but he was still testing and probing. I didn't mind going out with him in the city, no one ever knew you there, no one cared and best of all no one remembered. He always paid.

So when I told him the lie about the kids, he was right in and it was no trouble to get him to the house. I made it a nightfall jab, with the neighbours still glued to the TV and the blue lights flickering in every house round. He took right away to the typewriter Bee had in the bedroom, I let him stay there because the noise of it couldn't be heard next door and I could make sure he didn't go out. There was no kind of sense letting him be seen. As I watched him next morning settle down to bashing out a few more pages, all I could see was he was different from me. And above me, somehow. Or he thought he was. You could see it in the way he hunched over the machine, sort of hunched in prayer but also on the receiving end of a private line from someone up there that liked him.

He sat bare again, testing me. I can't say I didn't notice before how white he was, because I did, but one thing about him, he didn't smell at all. You can overlook a lot when someone doesn't smell or let his underwear go bad. It was just that I could feel him thinking that he had the upper hand on me. I couldn't care less about dominating someone— I don't need a side kick—but he cared. He wanted this book about me to be his book, he could see himself getting the glory, he was going to step high on my shoulders. If I let him. He was going to be the hero of it, not me. His name, in big print. I was something he picked up, soon he would drop me and pick up someone else. He was dominant. If I let him.

221

I didn't let him. I got the screwdriver that I'd ground down to an ice-pick point, put a felt guard on it up to the hilt to stop the squirting and put it in him while he sat there hunched. You could see his ribs easy, it was a snack to push it in between them. The guard worked fine and soaked up the red, but there wasn't much. His heart left home immediately. I held it in him until it looked as if the hole had stopped leaking, then put him in the bath to wash him. Don't any of you go grieving for him; you can't waste sorrow on people you don't know.

I burned the felt and washed the weapon, then concentrated on the body. I washed him again to get everything clean and hygienic and rinsed him so there was no soap left. The head, hands and feet were going to be the main worry, I didn't like messing with those parts of a person. I got a cardboard box, the one that came with the altar wine or the butter—I forget—and put the head in—his neck was pointed up the plug end, so he drained pretty easily. The bath water ran out under the house along a sort of rough drain that had board sides, and meandered into the rockery; the poinsettia might have redder colours next flowering.

I didn't mention the actual cutting because it's something that might worry people; I had to use Bee's breadknife and you have no idea how tough human meat is. It wants to stay joined together. And the sound is not something you should dwell on.

Touching the hands was better than hanging on to the feet while I sawed through. Somehow feet are more personal, they make you embarrassed easier. At that stage I had the head and two hands and two feet in the box. Just for the look of it, I changed their position and moved the head up to the top, hands in the middle and feet on the bottom. It didn't look good to have the feet sitting on the head. They had to be adjusted so that the cut part faced up, otherwise if they leaked down on bottom of the box and wet the cardboard, I might be in the position later of lifting the sides of the box and having the bottom stay on the ground along with the contents.

If I'd remembered my old man's cut-throat razor before, the job would have been easier. We still kept a little drawer half full of his things—all that was left of his forty-nine years. Books, shaving things, medals. With the razor I did a pretty good butcher's job on old Petersen and separated him into joints, chops, meaty ribs, and pieces of steak. At least I called them steak—they were the cheeks of his bottom, and his leg and thigh muscles. He didn't have enough arm muscles to call steak.

For the bones I had the old man's hacksaw, the one with the pistol grip. The meat I piled at the other end of the bath and let it finish draining. There was going to be some embarrassment with the bones later, but the meat would have to be finished first, no good getting rid of the bones bit by bit.

When everything was ready, I left the cardboard box in the bathroom and took the meat into the kitchen. I finished chopping it all up, wrapped it up with the lights and the skin in a cornsack, took the clothes and wrapped in them the contents of the cardboard box and left them in the barbecue grate. It was actually for burning rubbish, but we called it the barbecue.

That day I burned that part and stuck an old rubber tyre on the fire so no one would get the Auschwitz smell. And at night I borrowed a car and got down to the Zoo again and gave the cornsack to the lions. I had to go over the fence on the western side and be quick about it, because the animals kicked up a row. When I got back home and ditched the car and rubbed everything I touched with a gasoline rag, I checked that Petersen's extremities were burned up.

I had to pound up the bones with a hammer on the laundry floor and put them round the orange trees. Then I sat at the typewriter and slowly took over my story where Petersen had left it, just after he got to the house. I've chopped out a few of his comments where he went off the track a bit. You have to consider the readers, and you have to consider your own feelings, too. At least he didn't make my words come out differently; I checked through and they're as I told him.

He left a few scraps of paper along with the main story. One of them has on it; 'What feelings about violence he has used and sufferings caused to those robbed? Especially unfortunate drunks.'

I'd tell him, and I'll tell you now. None. No feelings at all. If they want to put themselves at a disadvantage, like rolling drunk, then walk out into the jungly old world, then they can take what comes. If it's a smack behind the ear and their wages gone, then so what? They can't do any better with their money than I can do with it. My kids are just as good as theirs.

Now Petersen can't know about it, I'll mention the money I saved up in the ceiling, out of all I got from drunks and others, over and above what I gave Bee. Bee and the kids would have enough to live on for a long while if I went away.

I hope no one's too disillusioned with me, or upset about Petersen, but I can tell you there's more people disappear than you know. Or the police admit. With luck no one would miss him, and there's very little noseyness round my way. It doesn't pay to shop anyone these days; someone like me can serve his time and still be out to even things up before the tattlers are much older.

Bee was back home the next week. She wondered a bit when she saw me there, but she didn't say anything. I didn't like to trick her with one of my sincere looks, so I tried to look pretty shifty. She was the same, though. Even while I was standing around pretending not to watch her, the house creaked from the heat and I felt a bit guilty. The kids were tired, Allie was asleep, and I was more or less useless, sitting there, looking out the windows, scaring myself a bit when I looked through the horizontal slats of the blind and found that the vertical binders were dancing all over the place, not just with every pulse beat, but in between as well. Bee trod very lightly, she hardly seemed to dent the floor mats, and all she did was for the kids. You could watch her and yet not watch, and it seemed as if she was put on earth one minute and straight away she began walking round getting things for people, fixing up the baby's mess, making little plans for taking the kids places and getting them things, making a cake for the woman next door that had her husband off work, shelling peas and slicing beans for the old lady that had arthritis in the fingers, but never doing what I did; I went there one day with the beans and saw what the old lady was doing. She had her hands in cold water half the day so I told her she ought to wake up to herself and use the rubber gloves Bee bought her, but she couldn't feel with gloves on; some stupid excuse like that. I told Bee she ought to stop doing things for her, but Bee didn't do what I said, or hardly ever, even though she mostly listened.

No matter what time of day she passed you, she was always fresh and she smelled light and sweet. I'd say all her underclothes were fresh on. I hate people that smell.

I tried to do a few things for her, mainly outside, but I soon got tired and had to sit down. After all, our house was the place where I'd been a little kid, from ten on, and there was a lot to think of. My cousin Jim visited us once years ago and I took him down the pitch to play cricket; he took the cover off my new six-stitcher in half an hour on the concrete wicket. That was just before he left to fight the communists. What I mean, he didn't exactly go to fight them, he was taken. He was only in the Army because he couldn't get a job.

Anyway, I was bowling to him, before the ball split, and when I tried to send down one he couldn't hit he yelled out that it swung a foot. Swung a foot? What did that mean? I didn't have a clue, but I thought he meant it was a seamer. I forgot all about it until one day I saw some cricket on the TV at home with Stevo and Bee. There was a bowler that swung the ball a foot and everyone said what a bowler he was. I didn't feel so bad about that cousin splitting my good ball then, in fact I think he meant to compliment me. He was captured later.

I went up the street to get a few refreshments for the family. A dog tried to chase me near a big house I used to deliver groceries to for old Cowan when he had the Post Office and general store, but this dog had never met me before. It tried to rush in and bite, then off. I grabbed for its neck but my hands slipped on its fur and all I got was the tail. You should have seen that dog sail through the air. Cats do that sort of thing much better, they keep their feet down, but this dog tumbled over and over like a sputnik. Luckily for the owner, it just missed a straight young ornamental tree. At that velocity, it would have broken the tree off at the roots, and it probably cost quite a few dollars. Dogs you can pick up in the street, but no one will let you pick up valuable trees.

Old whiskers used to trundle his barrow of vegetables up that street when I was a kid; it was funny to think that I could remember the exact spots I'd seen him and here he was, dead for years.

I took home a dozen bottles of beer, I had to get a taxi to carry them, I was getting puffed much sooner lately.

The kids liked their beer, it was good for their stomachs. Even Allie wasn't too young. All they had to remember if they got headaches was to have a big drink of water; that would dissolve their aches. I can tell you more about the family now there's no Petersen to get in the way.

Bee was fond of her beer and it was nice to have the whole family happily swallowing. I guess I was pretty clumsy, mainly because I was glad to see them all enjoying themselves together. Chris asked me later, 'Why can big people tread on your foot and not say sorry?' That was the first I knew that I had trodden on her. Even Stevo was able to look at problems of life and human existence after his second glass. He was looking at the wrinkles on his heel.

'Look, Mum. Afraid I'm getting old.' Bee laughed out loud. She always looked more cheerful after a glass of beer, until about the third one. Then she got to the stage where she doubted that she should be drinking beer at all. On the fourth, though, the world was right again.

'A boy is a boy,' she said, and it seemed a very deep thing to say. He was going for some sort of test the following Wednesday, I think it was an IQ test. We decided over the beer that he would do well.

The kids had wanted to have coloured sheets on their bed after they saw them in the shops and it wasn't long after that that I was able to give Bee enough money to get them. I won't tell you where the money came from, this time. When we got the sheets and Bee put them on the kids' beds, Stevo came out with; 'I'm glad I made those comments.' He made the original remarks about the sheets, it was only fair he should take the credit.

Bee asked Chris about the scripture class at Sunday school. 'What did you do at Sunday school, Chris?'

'I put some glue on Jesus.' I think Bee only asked her that to get one of Chris' funny sayings out of her, but we all appreciated it, even Stevo and little Allie, who laughed when she saw the others laugh.

It was nearly the same as when we looked in Stevo's book that he used at home for his sums. In the holidays they bring their old books home. You could find bits of notes any old time with the words 'I love Miss Thomson' in his shaky writing. He nearly went through the paper with each stroke.

It made me feel very good to be sitting there watching the beer take its effect on Bee. Actually the curve part of her eye where the eyelashes stick in was probably worth more than my whole sixteen and three-quarter years together, it was so beautiful.

She must have seen me watching her this time, because she was just at that stage of the beer where she could get mad over some little thing. She couldn't very well do anything to me, so she tore up some sheets of paper the kids had used for scribbling and acted mad that they'd been left around.

'Do you always tear up things when you're angry?' Chris asked. Bee saw reason then and smiled and the bad feeling passed. Those things always passed quickly in our house.

'I'm not really angry at them,' she said. 'I'm just on edge a bit, but how can you convince a kid of that?' She didn't want to have to tell me she'd caught me looking. I still can't understand why she was so sensitive about it.

She covered up a bit by getting back to the scripture classes; this time she asked Stevo how he liked them.

'They used to tell good stories but now they only tell you you're naughty.' Poor Stevo, the other kids were telling on him for playing under the bridge on the way to Sunday school and the big ones called him Herman Munster, he had big eyes and a crew cut. Bee tells me he's in trouble for chopping other kids with his hand.

Chris started then on a story about the kids at school and how one naughty little boy lifted up her dress and spat on her.

I wish they'd never had me. Out of millions of little wrigglers, why couldn't it have been someone else?

The kids seemed to be growing up and I was still only sixteen and three-quarters.

'There's a girl at school,' Chris went on, 'That I'm going to murder. She says, Stop pushing, little girl.'

Stevo had been thinking. He had slowed down, he had half a glass untouched.

'Mum, is it true there are some people you can never trust?' I suppose I had told him that, and it was only coming to the surface now, winkled out by the alcohol. We got him off the subject and started to sing a bit with Chris, Lay down yonder in the paw-paw patch, except that Bee made us sing Way down, instead of Lay down.

But even in the middle of singing I was thinking to myself, I wish I knew who took those photos of Ma's. Something in me wanted to be miserable. You could see Sydney out the kitchen window. From the distance the city's a big garden of hardy perennials, made of concrete, watered with money.

Something came up then that took me away from our little family meeting. I had to kill the black dog. Old Shieldsy had a black dog that was always making a pest of itself and for it to come round barking when we were happy was too much. Too much. I got the rifle and tied up next door's cat to the clothes line and waited under the house.

Sure enough, the black dog came and tried to torment the tied-up cat. I loosed two twenty-two slugs into it, but that didn't kill it outright. It was making a bad noise and dragging itself away into old Danny's place, so I picked up a rock about eighty pounds I reckon and let it fall on the black dog to slow it down, but it still kept making that bad noise, not so sharp and barky as before, but more moaning. I had to run back and get the axe to stop that noise, it was getting to me. The neighbours all kept inside.

I had to run a bit to catch up to the black dog, but it was worth it. Five or six overhead swings with the axe stopped the noise. I dragged the black dog by the feet down into the soft ground right down the back and buried him near where I tried to grow a potato patch. There was three feet of soil there before you hit the clay. He went in easy. When I got back near the house I put the rock back with the red side down on the ground. There was no sense upsetting Bee. There were no neighbours' heads in sight, I guess they heard the shots, but they were used to that.

'What did you do out there?' Bee said.

'I didn't do anything. Higgins did it.' I sat down as if nothing had happened, but all the time I had the bad feeling in my chest coming and going. It wasn't so violent, but it was there most of the time, as if the blood couldn't find the proper way round the circuit and was trying to bulldoze its way back in the wrong direction, and getting all tumbled and swirled about in the process.

I didn't let anyone see there was something going on. I told the kids the story about the white-foot cat with the black fur, he was a sort of hero among the cats we had, every day there'd be a big rat or a bandicoot brought up to the house with its insides missing. Every few sentences I had to stop a bit, there was something stopping the air getting into my chest. Maybe it wasn't the air, I'm not a doctor, but if it wasn't the air it was blood, and I was starving for it.

While I was going on about the famous black and white cat there was a sound of whistling like an eagle in the roof. In the mood I was in I was ready to think it was all sorts of things, but really I knew it was a possum. When they were bad in the roof, before Bee came there, they used to wet down through the ceiling and the smell was just like a human's when he's getting sick with something; it was a nutty, strong smell. I never forget smells.

Suddenly, sitting there with the kids and telling them stories and knowing I'd probably be there for a while if Bee didn't kick me out, I felt I could live forever. If only it wasn't for internal weaknesses. I hit my chest, though, and I could feel blood and things swirling around. I put the kids off, and helped Bee get them to bed. She was a colossal organiser and made allowance for my help, so I didn't feel I was in the way. Anyone else would have told me to shoot through.

A few distant shells out Ingleburn way whumped and thumped and made me think whether I would give everyone a break and join up, but when I thought how useless it was to be fighting for our government, with no one's heart in it and just shooting because the leaders couldn't think of anything more to say, I gave it away. It wasn't like one man going in and getting something out of it, shooting when he felt like it and stopping when he wanted to. Suppose it's

232

not very modern to hate teams and leaders, but that's the way of it. Maybe that's why I'm getting out of the crowds.

Bee was trying to take an interest in the world, at that stage. Always she had books around the place; I think she wasn't too satisfied with just going on living from day to day, she must have wanted to get out of the place, even if only inside a book. She nearly killed me with the expression on her face when I didn't know what Overkill meant.

Then she revived me with the sound of a tiny spoon chiming on her cup lip. I tried picking up her books and reading them, but I couldn't stand being glued in the one place for a long time; I could sit in the roof all night, but I couldn't read a book. I suppose it was because the book was trying to do something to me. I wouldn't have minded a book about some thin Australian hero dreaming of the bludging days gone by, standing in a pub, ordering 'Schooner a fifty...' That sort of thing.

She never said so, but I think she believed in progress and human betterment and all that. I think it's rubbish. We're no worse than our ancestors that stood stupidly at the mouth of a cave grumbling about the weather, but I reckon we haven't changed. We just do different things with our hands and say different words. I didn't say that to her, there was no sense in arguing with her for fun. There's a big enough wall between us now as it is.

I kept thinking, while I was cooped up inside the house, that I could hear a gate. I couldn't tell if it was opening or shutting. It was just making a noise. Maybe I should have taken its hint when I first heard it. When it came to clearing up the tea things I came across some pumpkin seeds; perhaps I should have gone outside and planted them and not come back. I planted them anyway; there seemed something so easy about putting living things in the dirt and going away knowing their life would take over and some time later there would be growing things to eat. All for just putting them in dirt, and giving them a drink of water.

We spoke together. She said, 'I want to finish that book.'

I said, 'Here, you better take your book.'

For some reason, she seemed pleased we spoke at the same time. It was a bit like old folks talking. It gave me a good feeling but I knew it wouldn't last.

For a while all I could hear was the sound of a book page. You know that dry, clean sound. I switched the TV on and saw the third movie I ever saw in my life, the Phantom of the Opera. That was years ago, and it was from right inside the theatre, not just underneath. I enjoyed that picture, because it made me glad to see poor Claude, all ugly through no fault of his own, scaring people to death and taking a beautiful girl down under the ground in a sort of cave. Boy, was I sorry to see him get it. So was a whole theatre full of other kids.

It wasn't so good on the TV, it didn't scare you a bit.

In the morning I hung round Stevo a bit, trying to hear the rest of the Chantic Bird story, but he snapped at me. I reckon he'd grown out of the Chantic Bird. Just when I was ready to hear it. Still, I guess he was waking up that you get no magic in this life; getting the big, rich, beautiful song out of the little grey bird is fairy story stuff.

They had the early TV on then and the last thing I remember Stevo saying was to the man in one of the ads; 'How would you know? You're only a puppet!' It was the same tone of voice he used to snap at me.

The next time I saw him he was riding half a mile away with Diana, his girl friend. They were on big chestnut horses, ambling around the district, going away.

I picked up one of his school compositions from the little shelf where he had his books, it was called

'A dead Lizid. In the holidays we went shooting rabbits.

In the way was a lizid. I shot him in the eye. He did a funny little dance before he was Dead.'

For some reason, I don't know, I folded the page and stuck it in my pocket. Now that I've given the kids a life and got them money, I can see them getting fatter and turning away from me. Or rather looking over my shoulder, past me at the world they think I stand for. I'll go before they start avoiding me.

This is nearly the end of that part of the story I'm going to let you hear about. It will be up and away for me soon. I know that in a lot of places there will be things I have left, things only I could have left. The world is not exactly as it was before me. That's something.

This funny memory is always with me. I can still see my brother in hospital, the same hospital where I had my appendix and tonsils out, and where we took Stevo for his burned leg. There was even an old man up one end of the James ward there dying at the same time as my young brother. It didn't seem right for an old cow like that to live so long, but at least he was cheerful and my brother was pretty miserable. It turned out to be a man we'd all given a lot of lip to when we were kids. He didn't seem to remember, though. I would have.

The next morning we had Allie in bed and the other kids at school when some of Bee's relatives came to the house. They knocked on the front door and since the main bedroom was in front we had to tumble out of bed and scat. Bee put on a dressing-gown and went to the door and told them she was in bed and not feeling very well and there was no news and the baby was asleep. I could hear from the way they spoke they suspected, but Bee got rid of them. I was sitting naked on the floor behind the door, you make less noise when you sit down, there's no bones to creak and you don't breathe so often.

A little kid came to the back door later on after a couple of eggs for its mother. I went for that one, without any clothes. The kid was too young to know, I reckon it had seen its father often enough not to worry. Bee's dog Puddin' was fighting with Stumpy, Stevo's lizard and Gubby, the she-cat from next door, but they made very little noise so I didn't worry Bee with it.

Now there's no interfering from Petersen, and he's out of the book, I can tell you what I was really hiding: one of the kids is our kid, Bee's and mine. Why should I tell old Petersen? I'd sooner have the rotten public know it than him, washing his hands in our private things. When Allie came, that was the only time I visited hospitals regularly. She was closer than parents and brothers. I'd see her in the viewing window, each day she'd be moved a place or two left, as more got born.

The worst thought I have now is that some day even my little Allie's eyes will let the darkness in.

If there is no other life, why is this one so lousy?

I did what I should have done a long time ago, and went after whoever it was that had been following me. At times I had thought it was imagination, but now I was sure there really was someone following me, watching, ready to pounce. Bee was reading a book about old British history and Boadicea and that gave me an idea about chariot wheels, so I got hold of another car from Russo's and welded a two inch pipe cross-ways near the back bumper, underneath the car to the chassis. I rigged up a steel bar that I could slide in the pipe by throwing a lever sideways in the car, a steel bar with an edge that could rip open a car, tyres and all. It didn't take me long to find the man that was following me. He was in a uniform, too, with a white shirt, tie and dark trousers. After I followed him a way I got ahead of him and came back the opposite direction. Russo's car was a Dodge this time and it stood its ground well when the steel ripped open my pursuer's car. Where it ripped along the side, the wind caught it and took it sideways right off the road.

That gave them something to think about when they found it. They could add that to their statistics. But people just don't understand that when bad things happen, it's someone like me paying them back.

No one looked like coming so I went to have a look at what I'd done. The side of the car had ripped and the wind had opened it up like a condensed milk tin and pushed it back sideways over the driver's head. Unfortunately for him the edge of it had half scalped him, the skin and hair was all lifted up loose and he was taking no notice when I got there. Have you ever noticed when you prang a car there's always rust under the paint? Rust under everything.

Somewhere it had gone wrong. This man didn't really look like he was following me, in fact allowing for the claret everywhere he looked a lot like a man I used to see on the train when I first went to work. I never spoke to him, but he just went to work and came back like all the rest. When you lived where we did and worked in the city, you always got home too late to do any work outside, if you were the kind that did that. And he did. I saw him with a fork or secateurs trying to make his garden the same as the other people in the street. And he did. There was no kind of point in a man like that following me. Actually he looked as if he might be just trying out his car, maybe he'd found a new thing to do instead of digging dirt. Tinkering with a car.

I got out of there feeling a bit bad. Ditched the car and wiped everything with a gasoline rag. No marks, no smells. Gasoline kills all smells.

Perhaps there had never been anyone following me. I must have made it up or something inside me had made it up because it knew I wanted to think someone was after me.

But there should have been someone following me, all the same. I had done enough for an army to be following me. In a way, I felt pretty cheated; it took from the excitement of the last few months.

One of my last actions in the house was to put the eye in new spirit and seal the lid so that it would keep forever in the ceiling. Or as long as forever is.

I decided about then to give the family bit away. Give them a rest. Like a sort of Adam that they taught us about in scripture at school, I had got kicked out of where I was put, I had to waste a bit of time mucking about with one thing and another, I had to get mixed up with a woman... Now, with the kids starting to grow away from me, I could move on.

I was sick of being at a loose end, I needed something to be attached to. Being free to go and do as you like isn't enough. I suppose going west isn't what you'd normally choose to do. Maybe I was called from over the hills. No. I've been pushed. Thinking there's been someone following me, not knowing who it is. I reckon it's me. Something inside me has to get away from the crowds into a place with more room to move, where you can't see so many people at any one time. I can manage a few at a time.

I decided to call it quits and look for something bigger. A town of my own, perhaps. I knew I could survive anywhere, all I needed now was to get some practice working through other people. I had to forget my habit of going alone all the time. I'd need a stooge or two. I didn't admit it to myself at the time, but Stevo snapping at me had rocked me. There was no point in staying on. Once when I thought it was like going away to die, I couldn't stop laughing.

A town of my own. Stolen cars, tow trucks, farm protection agent, local council, a town of my own. While the rest were looking upwards for bombs, I'd collapse them from inside.

I left the house after burning anything down the back-yard that might give a clue to who I was inside. All I left was a list of all the people I hate and I hid that. They would all get theirs some day.

The freesias were nearly finished, so up the street I wrenched out some freesia bulbs from the fence edges where they grew wild, sneaked back home and planted them. Next year Bee would be reminded of me.

On my way out past the pub, I followed a man with a good suit and rolled him when he got to his car. I got eighty-five dollars out of his pocket and left him on the back seat of his own car. A man with an open-neck shirt and a bit of grime on it came out before I left and went over to an old truck. I got him and only took half what he had. When I turned to go, something made me stop and go back and put some of the other man's money in the poor one's pocket. I walked out to the edge of the car park, but I couldn't make it. Something stronger took my legs back to the truck. I took the lot.

You won't believe how much the same it seems to me and all the kids I know; getting a man's job by competi-tion—or knocking him over the head.

This was my beginning. I felt so good I didn't mess their faces up, either of them, but round the corner I changed and wished I had, or at least put the boot in. I felt so rotten.

That night I slept in the mountains out past Kurrajong, where the switchback hills are, before Lithgow. Another coloured dream bored into my skull, this time I was in an old boat that was heavy in the water, I was so weak I couldn't move, and the boat was on fire. Just like the Viking funeral I once acted out for the fenced workers. Only this time I was blinded by the western sun and couldn't see if anyone was watching. Dying, I was, but weak, and no audience. There was no good feeling about it at all. I woke up almost in a sweat, except that I was cold. I always get cold in the mountains. The little dews on the grass had all the flashes of the ring I got for Bee, when you held it sideways to let the sun shine through.

I had a sort of vision that kept on in my skull. I got this picture in my mind of lots of little patches of Australia with no marks of human building on them, no tearing down, no ploughing—vacant patches, unused. Capable of being changed, worked, moulded. And tiny country towns. There must be hundreds of places just waiting for someone with a strong hand to take over. I would get a town for myself. Then when I had something behind me, another town. It can be done these days, people are weaker and more isolated from each other. They never get together now, their stupid competition for money and goodies takes up all their time, and separates them further from each other.

I spent all day there, getting some sun into me. The wind on my face there had crossed thousands of miles from the western ocean without being breathed by any other dirty human. There was no smoke from chimneys in it either. I was ready to go down out of the hills and onto the western plains to find a town to put in my pocket. I made a list of all the things I wanted and studied it for a few hours. I set off in the afternoon.

Looking at the hills in the late sunset, there was nothing as good as our world. Even if someone owns the hills—and that's always a bad taste in your mouth—they're still beautiful. Much the same way as Bee, the same quietness.

The Chantic Bird story isn't quite the same as Stevo left it. I went to a library and found that after the Bird had cured the King with her song and bargained for a sort of freedom, she volunteered, off her own bat, to become a spy for him if he kept her return a secret. She was going to tell him everything that went on in the country. I guess that cured me of Chantic Birds. By the way, it should be Enchanted Bird; Chantic was Stevo's own word.

I remembered a certain memorial on the road to Lithgow, that's why I took this picture with me from home and enough glue to stick it on with. It was a memorial to war and it always stuck in my throat that it was war, or actually gas, that laid the foundation for my old man's TB. Halfway down a hill into poor old Lithgow I stopped and glued my coloured picture of war. It was a man landing on Iwo Jima and one half of him was all right, but the other half had no uniform, no skin, no flesh, only shredded stuff. It was just before he fell on the sand. They don't allow that sort of stuff to be printed now—they're recruiting like mad—but just after the big war they let their heads go and showed all sorts of horrors.

I felt good, and sort of easy in my stomach after I glued it over their rising sun badge.

As I came down out of the mountains on to the plains,

it was funny how many times I got this rushing feeling in my chest. I try sitting up very straight, but it does no good. I have to have the vent windows turned right in, now, I just can't get enough air in my lungs.

As I finish this, I've stopped the car and got out, adding the last few lines to the story. Right now, nothing matters but living. I'll just leave the story—my story—on the back seat, I can't afford to let anyone read it yet. Slipping back over a few pages, what is it? A tale told by nobody. A mouth in the empty air. I wish this swirling pain in my chest would go away. When I take over my town I can't afford to have anyone see me doubled up like this, sweating like a pig in the cold country air. Trying to get breath into me.

Don't forget I'm writing to show you what a silly thing it is to live.

Text Classics

textclassics.com.au